COP KILLAS II, RENEWED JUSTICE

I0663734

This book is the fictional work of the author. Any likeness to any person living or dead is merely coincidental. All opinions expressed are solely those of the author.

ISBN: 978-1-945035-07-4

Edited by Black Lyfe Publications

Cover Design by Kranch Media

Printed in the United States of America

Cop Killas II

Renewed Justice

D. MANN

COP KILLAS II, RENEWED JUSTICE

Chapter 1

New Beginnings

It was a sunny Saturday afternoon and the mood was festive at Ms. Debra Williams Baldwin Hill's estate. The soul soothing sounds of 90's R&B glared from the giant concert speaker placed in the corner of the backyard.

92.3 The Beat radio station was jamming across the airwaves of Southern California this morning. Ms. Williams danced about with a youngness to match the era as Dana and Sharon egged her on. Crafty bullied the barbecue pit while smoking a blunt as DA and Pockets engaged in a fierce competition of skilled dominoes.

"Oh I got 'em in the graveyard," Pockets yelled, tossing back his glass of Hennessey. "He lookin' fa' bones, he lookin' fa' bones."

"You ain't did shit," DA retorted, twisting his lips while he continued to pull more dominoes. "You just giving me more ammunition to beat dat ass wit."

"Come wit' it my elder. Ass whoopin's are granted daily sir," Pockets teased, connecting his dominoes with a soft touch and uhh noise. "Get on round there! Get on round there!"

"DA! What I dun' told you about letting that young dude bully you on those bones?" Crafty yelled, blowing out a cloud of smoke. "I'm tired of it! You better hit 'em back right now dammit or yo' ass is on punishment."

The group roared with laughter as they studied the intense look on DA's face.

"He couldn't hit me wit' a Tommy gun if his name was John Dillinger," Pockets shot back, checking his imaginary watch for elapsing time. "Mannnnn! Study long, study wrong bruh. It's only gon' hurt for a minute, like a small needle in the ass. Let's not take all day sir. Let's not take all day."

DA studied the board comparing it to his hand. He looked like a lost child studying for a college exam on foreign language.

Crafty had the aroma of a certified grill master penetrating the nostrils of everyone within smelling distance. The beef ribs, links and chicken were inducing stomach rumblings that over shadowed the party. The group's faces were guided by instinct to the direction of Crafty.

COP KILLAS II, RENEWED JUSTICE

"Chef Boy Ar you'll never be," Pockets yelled. "When the grub gon' be done? Muthafucka hungry!"

"Will somebody put something in that boy's mouth?" Crafty urged. "I'm busy. Kick his ass DA! Damn."

Pockets ignored the comment by waving Crafty off with twisted lips.

"Take it like a man DA," Pockets spoke, teasing DA as he continued studying the dominoes. "Take it like a man."

Dana and Sharon took a seat next to one another watching Ms. Williams as she continued to float around the yard dancing. Moms or mama as the group now called Ms. Williams seemed so different over the last couple weeks since the murder of several officers and the chief of police.

Ms. Williams was more relaxed and her mood was pleasantly delightful on a daily basis, the death of those guilty officers seemingly brought her some much needed closure.

"Get it mama!" Dana cheered.

"You can tell mama used to dance a lot when she was young," Sharon confided. "She be moving girl."

The group watched in disbelief as Ms. Williams danced passed Crafty, snatched the lit blunt from between his lips and placed it between her own.

Ms. Williams was dragging hard on the blunt before the group could utter their first words of protest. They were waiting on her to choke but Ms. Williams held the smoke in like a pro; blowing it out with ease.

"I know y'all didn't think y'all were the only ones to ever smoke a joint," Moms stated, passing it to the still studying DA while she continued her dance trail around the yard.

"That's not a joint mama," Dana countered. "That's a blunt…and it's filled with that bomb ass Kush."

"Ooooh mama! You not supposed to be smoking," Sharon taunted, with a bright smile.

"HAHA! Fifteen on yo' monkey ass," DA screamed, slamming the domino with enjoyment while staring in the eyes of Pockets. "I need ten to go. Beeaaa!"

Pockets returned the glare with the most unimpressed look ever witness at a dominoes' table before calling his own twenty.

"Bolt the doors on the church house," Pockets yelled. "I'm throwing boulders when I end yo' career. Game over. Next! Beeaaa!"

"Fuck dat! You got lucky," DA replied, flipping and shaking the dominoes. "Run dat shit back!"

"Food ready!" Crafty interrupted, the busy group with his sound off alert. "I got dat shit smelling right."

"Whew! I'm starving," Pockets said, beginning his rise from the table.

"Where da' fuck you going?" DA inquired harshly. "We gotta game going on here."

"No. We had a game going," Pockets fired back. "You lost and I won. Let dat ass whoopin' hold until I finish eating. I'll be happy to beat up on you some more…a little later."

Pockets rose from the table and hurried towards the grill. Pockets intentionally irritated DA who stood directly behind him, by denying him the opportunity to avenge his loss.

"DAMMIT MANNN! Can we eat first?" Pockets responded, tired of the pressure DA was attempting to place on him. "GOTDAMN yo' brother thirsty! Nigga act like we dating or something."

"That's alright," DA spoke, blowing off the joke. "Imma date dat ass when I getchu' back on those bones."

"Fair warning bruh," Pockets said, turning and facing DA. "That shit sound real gay of you."

"Man fuck you," DA growled.

"I'm just saying dawg. Don't get mad at the messenger," Pockets stated. "Come in here sounding like Liberachi, I gotta to call you on that shit."

The group sat down to enjoy the grilled food while DA and Pockets continued to bump heads over the Domino game. Dana, Sharon and Crafty were busy licking fingers clean as Ms. Williams continued her care free waltz around the yard. She stopped dancing when she heard Crafty thinking out loud.

"I wonder if that commission shit the chief was talking about is true," Crafty said, stuffing his mouth full of barbeque ribs. "I don't think that fool was just talking."

"Me neither," DA answered. "His bitch ass did seem sincere as fuck, but I ain't never heard no mentioning of a commission anything."

"It don't mean he was lying," Pockets joined in. "Dude spoke that shit facing death."

"I thinks it's worth another look," Dana spoke, sipping on her drink and giving her two cents on the topic. "The police league is still in existence. Me and my baby just watched some TV special on dat shit little over a week ago. And the word commission flashed in and out sound so quick but we both caught that shit."

"I think it's time we stop talking about the past," Ms. Williams interjected. "It's my off day, I'm with my family and y'all about to ruin my buzz with this conversation. Crafty! Since you started it, you can refill my drink."

"Yes ma'am," Crafty agreed, wiping his fingers and grabbing Ms. Williams's empty glass before stepping away from the table.

"Now that's enough of that talk. Let's eat, be merry and celebrate like it's no tomorrow," Ms. Williams advised, dancing back off onto her own sunset. "We have plenty time left for that conversation."

DA was threw with the conversation for the moment, but the issue re-sparked his interest. This wasn't over by a long shot.

"Pockets. Help me grab something outta' the car bruh?" DA asked, rising from the table.

Pockets looked on strangely until he noticed the slight head nod from DA. Pockets rose from the table and followed DA through the massive house, out to the driveway.

"Get in," DA instructed, hitting the alarm to his truck, automatically unlocking both doors.

"Wassup," Pockets questioned, sliding in the seat and closing the door.

"It feels weird asking yo' opinion," DA started, with a pause and deep breath. "But sometimes that dumb ass intelligent shit you be spitting be on point. So I have to ask man, what you think about that commission shit for real?"

"Nigga was that a compliment or an insult! Shit," Pockets retorted. "Thanks for the compliment, fuck you for the insult."

"Nakarebeeshwa," DA announced.

"WHAT!" Pockets fired back.

"That's Swahili for you welcome," DA replied.

"Look here nigga, stop trying to get bright on me ok," Pockets shot back. "Just keep it dumb and American, shit be simple that way."

"Shit be simple that way," DA mimicked. "Anyways whatchu' think about that commission bullshit honestly?"

"Just my like my lady said; shit worth an investigation," Pockets responded. "In fact after we watched that show on TV last week. I been on my Sherlock Holmes and guess what I found out…that shit really existed back then."

"Fuck outta here. How da' fuck you find out and I got paid experts who ain't found out shit yet?" DA barked.

"Maybe I should be on the payroll then," Pockets said, reaching and pulling a folded piece of paper from his back pants pocket. "Here. I was gon' show it to everyone together but then moms tripped out."

DA studied the paper with intense scrutiny. "I'll be damn. Where you get this from?"

"I copied it from the internet, deep out the archives," Pockets told.

DA glanced over at Pockets thinking he was right, Pockets should be on the payroll. DA perused the paper for a few more seconds before laying the paper in his lap. He sat back quietly thinking to himself.

"I swear I'm firing me a muthafucka first thing in da' morning," DA announced, giving himself and Pockets a brief giggle. "So this shit really did exist."

"That's the only piece of evidence I found showing the commission existed in more than of week of searching," Pockets admitted. "And you see it don't say shit on it except they met on that day."

"That's all it needed to say. Damn. I owe you one," DA conveyed. "Thanks bruh. Aye who the whites dudes on the picture?"

"The tall dude was the chief when he was younger," Pockets indicated, pointing at the sheet of paper. "Don't know who the other dude is. And check this out, your boy o' chief was a member of the police league too."

"Doesn't even surprise me. Damn," DA murmured, staring back at the photo, with a growing smirk. "The chief aged fucked up."

"Yeah he did. C'mon, let's go back in before they come looking for us," Pockets advised.

The two men climbed out of the truck and headed back to the party with promises of taking that topic up later.

"I see you just like pretending to be an idiot huh," DA stated, following Pockets back through the house.

"Yeah. I figure it'll strengthen our relationship since you like pretending to be smart," Pockets replied. "And now, soon as we touch those bones, I'm gon' beat on you like cracka' ass slave master. No sympathy DA. None at all sir."

"Just don't pencil whip me bruh," DA argued. "And this time I'm keeping score…cheating ass."

The two men returned to the festive party. Dana, Sharon and Ms. Williams danced a circle around Crafty as they enjoyed *The O' Jays, For the Love of Money*. Pockets quickly joined the dancing group as the euphoria raged on. DA sat back at the table and poured himself another drink. His mind wasn't on the party, it was on the commission and police league.

Crafty spied his homeboy at the table apparently in deep thought, he knew just where DA's mind was at. It was on the Commission! Crafty watched as DA pulled his cellphone, made a brief call and hung up. Crafty made his way over to the table and took a seat next to DA.

"Wassup bruh? You thinking about that commission shit huh?" Crafty asked.

"A little bit," DA admitted, shaking his head back to reality. "Aye in an hour imma need you to roll with me. I wanna check something out."

"Fa' sho," Crafty answered, swallowing the rest of his drink and rejoining the dance line.

The group begged DA to come dance but he declined time and time again, until Sharon personally dragged him from the table and engaged him in a two-step. They danced for the next hour.

The family continued to party, drink and eat. DA excused himself and Crafty with the excuse of making a beer run. They had passed nearly fifty liquor stores enroute to their destination.

"Where we going?" Crafty asked, looking at the downtown skyline.

"You'll know in a minute," DA replied.

DA pulled the truck into the garage of the ten story building and parked. Crafty knew exactly what they were doing there now.

"I don't see his little sports car at all," DA exclaimed, performing a quick visual inspection of the surrounding area.

"Here he come now," Crafty cautioned, now understanding the who, what and why of their unscheduled visit.

The two men sat back quietly sharing a blunt. DA had parked in the far corner to remain unnoticed. They watched the man rise from his low sport car, grab his briefcase and head for the elevator doors.

"Dude look a little spooked to me," Crafty advised. "I wonder what his problem is."

"Yeah his ass do look nervous," DA replied, watching the man board the elevator while smashing the blunt in the ashtray. "C'mon. Let's see what's got this dude so shook up."

DA and Crafty exited the vehicle and walked to the elevator doors. They entered the elevator and DA pushed the button for the six floor.

The doors opened and the man stood there fumbling with papers he attempted to stuff in his briefcase. The man glanced up in time to witness DA arms snatch him into the elevator.

"Back down!" DA called out, signaling Crafty to their next location. "Eddie, Eddie, Eddie. What's goin' on man? You making a brother feel pretty unimportant these days, especially after I paid you my money. Where you been hiding lately?"

"Get your fucking hands off me brute and the name is Edward," the man responded.

"Damn that's a switch. What's got you so uptight and in a rush?" DA questioned, straightening the man's jacket collar back into position.

"I don't know what you've gotten yourself into but you'd be wise to leave it alone now," Edward warned. "Some powerful people got upset about that simple inquiry into the Commission and now I'm receiving visit from unidentified strangers. I'm not asking another question about the Commission and I'm leaving town pronto."

"What strangers?" DA roared.

"Don't know. They never identified themselves," Edwards proclaimed. "But they sure as hell as look official and downright evil."

"I give a fuck how they look! What the fuck they wanna know about?" DA yelled.

"Ooh, they didn't come to find out anything. They came with a message," Edward disclosed. "Stop snooping or else. I think I'm gon' take that advice, it seems sound…and you should do the same. You're definitely receiving a full refund."

The doors of the elevator opened and Edward walked away repeating his warning for DA to let this commission thing be a dead topic. DA wasn't taking advice today or any other day, he was just getting started with his probe.

Chapter 2

Street Races

DA sat on the phone waiting to be connected. He had been looking for two other information brokers that he employed to research the commission group.

"Something's wrong," DA spoke, sighing. "Neither one of these dudes was at the office yesterday and neither one of 'em answering today."

Sharon sat back thinking. "You think its foul play? Edward did say yesterday that some evil, official looking goons popped up. Maybe it's connected."

"It wouldn't surprise me," DA mentioned, sliding out of the bed and heading to the bathroom. "You going into work this morning or you wanna make a couple runs with me?"

"I'd rather have you crawl back in this bed and finish what you started this morning," Sharon answered.

Sharon pushed the sheet covering the lower half of her body pass her ankles, and exposed her nakedness.

COP KILLAS II, RENEWED JUSTICE

DA simply stared with a smile across his face. It took a second for him to snap back to the world before he gave his reply.

"Get yo' fine ass outta bed. Its business time," DA ordered, watching Sharon's movements like a hungry wolf.

DA needed a release and Sharon had offered her love earlier this morning, DA accepted and ravaged her given passions. It was time for work now.

Sharon crawled out of bed, swaying her naked body pass DA standing in the bathroom doorway. He could feel himself getting excited as he slapped her buttock and watched it jiggle. Sharon looked down and noticed DA's excitement also. She grabbed his member, pulling him into the shower.

"I could be doing a follow up to an inquiry I made into the police league," Sharon told. "Or I could doing you."

"Its business time," DA uttered, giving a quick reminder to Sharon who was massaging his extension with passion.

DA spun around, turning the knob and let the water rain down over his physique. He quickly began to lather up to Sharon's vocal disapproval.

"That's not fair DA," Sharon protested, wrapping her arms across his chest and hugging DA from behind. "I give it you when you want it."

DA began singing his one repeated line, *business; I just wanna do business*.

"That's cool," Sharon whispered, in his ear. "Just don't get mad when I wanna do business. I'm not doing nothing but business."

DA smiled knowing Sharon could never hold her word when it concerned him. He finished showering, stepped out and started getting dressed. He waited for Sharon in the truck.

DA was in full business mode by the time Sharon climbed in the truck and closed the door. DA shifted the truck into drive, pulled out the garage and floored the gas pedal racing along the streets.

"Hello. Hello," DA repeated, into his phone while he traveled northbound on La Brea Ave. "Got damn! I keep getting his voicemail."

"Calm down babe. Its gon' be alright," Sharon suggested, rubbing his shoulder. She could tell something had him bothered. "You'll find what you're looking for."

COP KILLAS II, RENEWED JUSTICE

DA remained quiet letting his thoughts fashion his next move. He made a left turn and pulled into Roscoe's Chicken and Waffles parking lot.

"Let's eat," DA instructed, sliding out of his seat.

Sharon followed and the two walked in to the establishment. A waitress escorted the couple to a table near the back, gave them menus and disappeared.

DA scanned the restaurant's patrons while in deep thought. Sharon fiddled with her phone for the next five minutes while she and DA waited on the return of the waitress. The waitress returned, placing two glasses of water on the table and began taking their orders.

As the waitress walked away, DA took notice of a man coming directly down his aisle. The man was white, short, heavy set and wore those super dark cop glasses. The man walked passed DA and into the restroom.

"You see this dude just walked pass," DA alerted, tapping Sharon's arm.

Even with dark glasses on DA felt the man's glare attempt to penetrate his soul. DA was a lot more attentive to the guy when he came out of the restroom, checking everything he could about the man.

D. MANN

DA stared the short man down, watching the man as he walked out of the restaurant. DA thought that was kind of strange, he had never witnessed exactly where the man had come from and now the man was gone.

"He looks ex-something," Sharon advised, staring the man down as he came and left. "Ex-agent, ex-military, ex-officer; he ex-something for sure."

DA chalked up the strangeness to him being overly suspicious. The news from Edward had spooked DA a little and DA chuckled to himself when he recognized it.

Gotta get my shit together, DA thought to himself. He pulled his cellphone from its holster and began making calls again. DA's irritation grew as the phone continued to ring. Again, there was no answer. DA took a deep breath trying to ease his mind, he hated unanswered questions. DA tried another number with the same result.

"Fuck!" DA muttered.

"You sure you're alright? You've been pissed off since I got in the truck," Sharon inquired. "I didn't do anything, did I?"

"Naw. I'm just tryna' find these brokers," DA replied, shifting his thoughts again.

DA scrolled through his phone's contacts and tapped the screen.

"Hey wassup," DA spoke, into the phone before going silent.

The waitress came and placed their food on the table. She asked if they needed anything else. DA rudely hand gestured the woman away struggling to hear his phone conversation. The waitress frowned and hustled off to serve another customer.

"Nothing!" DA repeated, in a quick muffled tone, taking another breather. "Yeah I holler atchu' later."

DA placed the phone back in its holster and prepared to throw down on the breakfast that sat in front of him, Sharon was already forking through hers.

"So what you have on the agenda for the day?" Sharon questioned, making light conversation as they ate.

"Once we leave here, we finna' snatch up Crafty and then I need you to do some hunting for me," DA told.

"Hunting," Sharon questioned, with surprise written across her face. "For what?"

"Exactly what you're doing already; that police league," DA mentioned.

"Pockets actually found a news story from back in the day that proves the commission existed. I'm certain these police league and commission dudes ran together. Finding one could lead us to both," DA confided. "You think you can use your connections to dig up something quietly?"

"Yeah no problem," Sharon answered. "I gotta source or two inside."

"Hey," DA called, grabbing Sharon's wrist to beckon her attention. "The key word is quietly. Two dudes already missing in action and I don't need to worry about you disappearing too."

Sharon smiled at the suggestion that DA was concerned about her safety. She wanted to jump across the table and make love to him at that very moment. DA mustered up enough strength to crack a smile at the sight of hers shining so brightly.

"What?" DA asked, with his smile still plastered on his face.

"Nothing," Sharon responded, locking eyes with the man she loved. "I just love you baby."

Sharon watched as DA blushed returning her sentiments. The couple finished their meals and DA left the waitress a generous tip.

The couple were traveling to Crafty's house when Sharon put down her phone and peered at traffic through her side view mirror. Her stare became intense.

"We gotta tail," Sharon spoke, alerting DA of a car following them.

"What!" DA yelled, cynically raising only his eyes to view the car through his rear-view mirror.

"Seven cars back, grey sedan, two occupants," Sharon called out, identifying the suspects. "They've been with us for the last two blocks, turn for turn."

"We'll see right now," DA said, merging across the lanes and making a right turn at the corner. "Let's see if they hit this corner wit' us."

"They're still there," Sharon warned, spying their movements and drawing her weapon from her purse.

DA turned another two corners before pulling into a gas station. He grabbed his Glock pistol and stepped out of his truck.

D. MANN

DA stood behind his open door, pistol to his side waiting on their pursuer's arrival. DA gripped his weapon tightly as he spotted the grey sedan turning the corner. Sharon stood with her door opened and gun in hand. She and DA both watched anxiously as the grey sedan turned the corner and continued to pass on by.

Both occupants of the grey sedan turned their faces as they cruised by. DA and Sharon were focused like eagles on the passing car. DA in a hurried movement, climbed back in the car, racing out of the station.

"You see dat shit! Both of them muthafuckas turned their heads when they passed us," DA expressed, with conviction.

"Looks like their trying to avoid detection," Sharon recalled.

"Oh well. They won't be avoiding that shit today," DA alerted.

"What are you doing?" Sharon asked, fastening her seatbelt.

"Following these bitches. See where the fuck they going," DA admitted, smashing his accelerator to the floor and speeding through traffic to catch up to the other vehicle.

DA managed to get three cars behind the sedan before the sedan accelerated, bobbing and weaving wildly in and out of traffic.

The chase was on!

DA gave pursuit, pushing his truck's engine unlike ever before.

"They're getting away baby!" Sharon yelled, pounding on the truck's dashboard. "Get 'em baby! Get 'em!"

"I got these coward ass fuckas," DA reassured, turning the corner slightly on two wheels and screeching tires. "They ain't getting away."

"Oh shit baby be careful!" Sharon screamed, feeling the truck rock from side to side before launching forward.

"I got it!" DA yelled, wrestling the steering wheel back into position. "That muthafuckin' cracka driving the shit outta that car...but imma catch his ass."

"Damn, he is driving the hell outta that car," Sharon admitted, watching with big eyes as the sedan nearly missed colliding with a big rig truck. "You see that shit?"

"Hell yeah. I thought he was through with money," DA replied, giving more horsepower to his engine.

"You on 'em baby!" Sharon said. "Try and get on the side of them!"

The near accident between the sedan and the big rig truck allowed DA enough time to catch up to the sedan. The sedan raced along swaying from side to side trying not to allow DA to pull alongside of it. The two vehicles were now bumping each other frequently.

"O' this dude wanna play bumper cars huh," DA uttered, slamming the much bigger Chevy Suburban against the rear quarter panel of the sedan. "Trying to make us crash, okay muthafucka you about to recognize."

The driver of the sedan nearly avoided being the victim of the *Pit Maneuver*. The sedan switched lanes to the opposite side of the street and rocketed forward into oncoming traffic. Cars went screeching into all other lanes causing numerous accidents to occur within seconds and right in front of DA's truck as he barely missed car after car.

"Again! Do you see this muthafucka?" DA screamed, glancing over quickly at Sharon. "He showing absolutely no consideration for public safety. Promise me that we whooping his ass Rodney King style when we catch 'em.''

"I promise baby," Sharon agreed.

"This is one of those moments when I feel like crying," DA admitted, while navigating through the frenzy the white driver was causing.

"Why?" Sharon asked, quizzically.

"Cause' I gotchu' with me right now; I'm technically the law," DA started. "And now I get to whoop a cop ass for running from me. Sweet irony always brings a tear to my eye baby."

Sharon smiled and screamed almost simultaneously. "DA watch out!"

An old homeless man dragging a shopping cart full of his belongings entered the crosswalk of the intersection without a look or seemingly a care. DA's truck swerved missing the homeless man by inches. The truck ripped the cart from the man's hands obliterating it into small pieces, strewn across the intersection. DA's sudden swerve sent him and Sharon uncontrolled over the edge of a curve and spinning in a donut.

"AHHHH!" the two screamed, in unisons bracing for impact.

Pedestrians went scrambling from the corner as the black suburban went careening into the street light located on the corner.

Errrrrrrrrrr! Bammmm!

The Suburban smashed into the light pole sending debris flying in every direction. The jolt bobbled the couple around inside the truck.

People rushed over to see if the two were alright, attempting to snatch the truck doors open. DA looked over concerned, questioning Sharon about her physical status; she was alright. DA and Sharon looked on as the sedan made a left turn at the corner and disappeared from sight.

"Fuck! Almost had dem' muthafuckas," DA yelled, visibly frustrated.

DA pushed the door open and staggered out of the truck, he laid against it trying to re-gather himself. He was met by the old angry homeless man and a ton of swinging fist.

"You destroyed my home you son of a bitch!" The old man screamed, throwing punch after punch and kick after kick. "You fucking idiot!"

"Calm down old dude!" DA yelled, grabbing the elder to control him. "I'll take care of it! I'll take care of it."

COP KILLAS II, RENEWED JUSTICE

DA found himself tussling with the elder until Sharon came around the truck and announced herself as an officer of the law.

"Calm down sir! I'm a detective," Sharon advised. "We'll rectify the situation."

"Goddamned right you're gonna rec...rec...fix the goddamn situation," the old man yelled, starting to let his anger subside.

DA let the old man go and checked on the condition of his truck. The front was destroyed. DA called the tow truck service and Crafty to come pick him and Sharon up. He gave the old homeless man the nine hundred dollars he had in his pocket and promised that he would return to further repay the elder.

Chapter 3

Double O Negro

Crafty and Pockets sat inside of DA's new black Range Rover awaiting his return. They were parked in a deserted lot of what appeared to be old, abandoned warehouses.

There was old rusted cars and car frames everywhere. Stacks of piled steel, eight feet high littered the old cracked cement sections. The weeds were overgrown and swallowing whole objects.

The buildings looked dilapidated. Worn paint and broken windows gave it a ghostly makeover. The place had an eerie feeling that surrounded it and it was making both men uncomfortable waiting around. It gave Pockets the vision of a haunted steel mill.

"He been in there for a while now," Crafty stated, seeming concerned. "And this nigga out here in no man's land hiding like a bitch. Anything could happen to a muthafucka out here and wouldn't nobody know shit."

"I'm on the lap wit' mines," Pockets uttered, cocking back on the chambers of his twin nine millimeter pistols. "Anything look funny and I'm poppin' til' I'm empty."

The advice was subtle, but Crafty heeded the warning. He pulled his own pistol, cocked it back and laid it across his lap. He did his next pistol the same way.

"My nigga ain't outta there in the next three minutes; I'm going in," Crafty warned, staring at the door DA went through. "I know he told you about that shit that happen to him and Sharon this morning."

"Just chill people," Pockets urged, performing a quick scan of the surrounding area. "That's a big ass dude, he can take care of himself."

"Yeah you right," Crafty conceded. "Still…if the homie ain't outta there in the next few, I'm going in."

"Fuck it. I guess I'm going in witchu' then," Pockets agreed.

The men sat quietly for the next couple minutes surveying the area. DA and another man stepped outside and shook hands. DA and the man had a few more words before DA headed back to the truck. The man sat in front of the door watching the group as they readied themselves to leave.

Pockets noticed the movement between the abandoned cars first and started to notify the group when the first shots rang out, smashing through the driver's side windows.

"It's a hit!" Pockets yelled, grabbing the side of his face and falling out of the truck.

"Aww shit! Pockets hit!" DA screamed, returning fire. He struggled as he scurried across the console and slid out of the truck's passenger side door.

Crafty fired shots out the shattered window as he squirmed out of the back seat on the passenger's side.

DA's new truck took shell after shell. DA fell out the truck, looking around feverishly but couldn't locate Pockets. Crafty landed next to DA as they took cover and returned fire.

"Where the hell is Pockets?" Crafty screamed, firing off four consecutive shots.

"I don't know," DA answered, firing off several rounds himself.

"Who da' fuck shooting at us?" Crafty questioned, emptying his first clip.

"Don't know that either," DA replied, squeezing off more rounds.

COP KILLAS II, RENEWED JUSTICE

Crafty took a second to reload and noticed the man DA had been talking lying dead in the doorway of the warehouse. Crafty re-took his position at the back of the truck glaring for the enemy.

"They knocked yo' boy down," Crafty told. "He laid out in the doorway."

DA ducked down glancing behind himself to see his associate lying dead.

"Damn!" DA growled, returning shots to the armed assassins. "Where the fuck is Pockets at?"

"They got us pinned down homie and I'm getting low on ammo," Crafty yelled, through the continuous gunfire as he fired both pistols at their attackers.

DA checked his ammunition, he had only one clip left. He and Crafty had to move away from the range rover; it was being shredded by bullets.

DA knew the truck wouldn't stand much more. He spied the area and saw their next position, a stack of steel piled about five feet high but nearly fifteen feet away.

In a gunfight, fifteen feet away was equivalent to the hundred yards on a football field.

"Crafty!" DA barked, already pointing in the stack's direction. "We have to get to that steel stack over there. Get ready to cover me."

Crafty moved from the rear of the truck to the front, next to DA and took position. Both men were peeking over the hood ready to make their move when they noticed Pockets maneuvering the maze of junk cars at full speed.

Pockets' movements were gazelle-like as he launched himself head first over a rusted car frame landing in a frontal tug roll. His landing was a perfect 10 as he rolled forward to his feet, rose with both guns extended to full arm's length and walked out of the motion firing both pistols, killing two assassins by head shots.

"Y'all fuckin' witda' wrong one!" Pockets screamed, at the two dead men.

The commotion alerted the other three assassins who were now honing their guns in Pocket's direction. Pockets rolled to side and disappeared.

The assassins searched nervously moving in the direction that Pockets was last seen. With Pockets on the loose and the assassins hunting him, it presented the perfect timing for DA and Crafty to advance their own position.

COP KILLAS II, RENEWED JUSTICE

The two moved quickly, getting around to the backside of the assassins who were searching through the area of countless steel stacks.

DA and Crafty split up to box in the remaining killers. DA decided to take a bird's eye view of the situation and climbed atop of a steel stack. He could see along several rows as he moved along the beams. Crafty stayed on the ground.

DA spotted an assassin and knelt, taking careful aim. He was just about to pull the trigger when Pockets emerged from between steel stacks snatching the gun from the man's hand and giving him a full body spinning elbow in one motion. Pockets caught the assassin's jawline perfectly sending him tilting like the Tower of Pisa. The assassin's head caught the steel stack on his way to the floor making a *Tink* sound. The assassin was unconscious when Pockets fired a single shell into his head. Pockets nodded at DA and disappeared again.

DA jumped off the stack and crossed two aisles over. He climbed atop another stack and moved along it quietly. He could see Crafty creeping forward right below him, searching every possible hiding place.

Both men were caught off guard when gunfire rang out, spraying in Crafty's direction. Crafty attempting to jump backwards, stumbled over debris and fell on his backside. It actually saved him! Crafty could hear the shells whiz pass his head as he was falling backwards.

DA yelled out for Crafty and the assassin stepped from between the steel stacks, backing up as he took aim at the top of the stack. The assassin thought he had killed Crafty, he was hunting DA now.

The assassin shuffled along sideways never taking his eyes off the top of the stack. It wasn't until the assassin glanced down while passing Crafty's body, did he see the Glock pistol in Crafty's hand.

"Oooh shit!" The man exclaimed, witnessing Crafty's growing smile.

"Yeah you fucked up," Crafty shot back.

Crafty fired off several shots backing the assassin into the steel stack directly across from them. DA popped up atop the stack and gave the man several shots to the face. The assassin's body slid down to the floor; he was gone.

"It's looks to be only one of you left," DA yelled, walking upright and slapping his pistol against the side of his leg. "Come out, come out wherever you are."

COP KILLAS II, RENEWED JUSTICE

"His ass ain't coming out nowhere," Pockets echoed. "But you can come get his sorry ass."

DA looked down at Crafty in bewilderment. He gave a slight smile and a chuckle. They could hear what seemed like faint, muffled sounds of agony in the distance.

"This little dude took down four of these fools," DA stated, jumping off the stack and walking with Crafty to Pocket's location.

"I still don't believe that shit and I saw with my own eyes," Crafty added.

DA and Crafty walked to the end of the stacks and made a right turn. The assassin was on his knees breathing heavy with Pockets hovering over him, holding a pistol to the top of his head. The assassin had two black eyes, a bloody nose and a busted mouth.

"Damn! You did all that to him?" Crafty asked.

"I asked him a couple of questions nicely but dis' muthafucka wanna be hard about it," Pockets replied. "You know how that shit go."

"So what he tell you so far?" DA asked.

"Pleeeeeze! Pleeeeeze! I'm sorrrrry! Don't hurt meeeeee!" Pockets sang, in a whimpering tone.

"Some shit like that, I wasn't tryna' hear dat shit doe."

"Who are you? Who sent you? Who you work for?" DA asked, the bleeding man.

DA got no response.

"He have any I.D on 'em?" DA inquired.

"Nothing," Pockets responded. "No wallet, no papers, no jewelry. Nothing, not even fuckin' initials."

"So you not talking huh?" DA asked, the man. "A soldier to the end. I can honor that. A soldier dies but once, a coward dies a thousand deaths. Ain't that how it goes? That is the cliché right?"

The man kept eyes down and his mouth closed.

"Don't worry. I'm sure they'll tell your wife and kids that you died in some heroic fashion serving your country. That's the usual lie they tell to comfort your family once you're gone," DA teased. "Hell, with you out here doing this kinda shit, I'm sure you have a buddy out there somewhere waiting to console your lonely ass wife."

The man finally glared upwards at DA.

"Oh he soft right there," DA acknowledged. "What? Wifey getting the pipe while you out murdering."

The man lowered his eyes back to ground level.

"She getting that black pipe ain't she?" Crafty interrupted. "You know them freaky ass white girls love that black pipe."

The man looked up with a smirk this time.

"I would fuck her," Pockets joined in. But I dislike that flat, soggy, dog smelling, rotten ass white meat. Doctors say that shit bad for my black systcm."

"Fuck it!" Crafty interjected, stepping closer to the assassin and touching the tip of his pistol to the man's head. "If he not gon' talk, minds well put a bullet in his head."

"Promise to spare my life and I'll tell you what you wanna know," the assassin pleaded.

"Oh he talks," DA mocked.

"I already told you that," Pockets argued. "Earlier it was just *pleeeeeze, pleeeeeze, pleeeeeze*. I thought the cracka' was giving me his rendition of James Brown."

"You gotta deal. Start talking," DA commanded.

The man glanced upward looking sorrowful.

"Silence is a deal breaker. Tell me something," DA urged.

"We were sent here to record and monitor Jonah's activities," The man started. "If he spoke to anyone about sensitive information, we were order to eliminate any possible threats. You guys became that threat when you pulled up."

"You said record. How?" DA asked.

"We have a van on the north side of the yard," the man answered. "We've been monitoring what little communications he used. We must have missed your incoming call because you shocked everyone when you arrived. We couldn't I.D you because you have dealer's plates on your truck, so we waited for your departure.

"You look young. You a new booty? Who you work for?" Pockets asked, slapping the man in the top of his head with his pistol.

"We never know," the man grunted, pinching his head between his shoulders in reaction to the slap he received. "We get our orders through a secure communication link, a wire transfer deposits our money into an account and we go to work."

"Mercenaries. Nothing but paid killers," Crafty uttered, in disgust.

"I work for the interest of national security," the man said.

Pockets stood behind the man with his pistol raised directly over the man's head. Pockets nodded his question to DA, DA nodded his answer back.

"Hey white boy," Pockets called, circling around to the front of the man.

The young white man looked up to see that his fate had been sealed. He mustered up the strength to die with some dignity. He tilted his head back and stuck his chest out.

"You fired," Pockets stated, pulling the trigger in the face of the young white man and killing him instantly.

"Can you believe this muthafucka' tryna' die like a soldier," Crafty asked. "Sticking his chest out, hmmm."

"They'll die for that great white hero shit in a minute," Pockets added.

"He was gassed up on those bullshit white supremacy lies," DA told, while laughing. "I bet he's in hell right now filling out a request form for ice."

"Hell yeah," Crafty added, with a loud laugh. "Aye we need to go search those other dudes befo' we get up outta here."

The crew nodded in agreement. They headed back the way they came, searching the dead men's bodies for identification or whatever. They found the keys to the van but no I.D on any of them.

The crew headed for the north side of the yard in search of the would-be killer's van. They found it parked next to a huge column that supported a no longer used train bridge. The men opened all three doors of the van and began searching. They didn't find anything that disclosed the killer's identity but they did find a gold mine in a weapons cache and surveillance equipment.

"Damn goon squad had heat," Crafty muttered, searching through the metal crate. He fingered the numerous automatic assault rifles and grenades. "I'm glad they thought we were nobodies."

"Naw it wasn't that, they just didn't know we had double-o negro wit' us," DA returned, shaking his head in amazement. "At least we have one problem solved."

"Yeah," Pockets said, questioning DA's statement. "What's that?"

"We know how we getting home now cause' my truck is fucked," DA answered. "And I just paid a grip fa' dat fucka."

"Suck it up rich guy," Crafty advised, strolling around to the driver's side door where DA was located and slapping him on the back. "We got bigger problems than that."

"Like what?" DA inquired, bewildered.

"Whenever these fools don't report in," Crafty started, making sure to eye Pockets standing in the passenger side door. "Whoever paid these goons, gon' send more of 'em to try and kill us. I suggest we get the fuck up outta' here."

"Good suggestion but they wasn't looking for us. Remember they were watching Jonah," DA reminded, the two.

"Yeah," Crafty agreed, climbing in the truck and taking a seat in the back row. He was now checking through the surveillance equipment. "But still, let's get the fuck outta here."

"So wassup witda' other dude you had checking shit out? You still ain't heard shit from him yet?"

Pockets asked, closing the passenger's door behind him.

"Naw. Not a word," DA replied, closing his door and turning the ignition key. "It wouldn't surprise me if he was dead now, scared or running. Shiid, they killed Jonah and spook the hell out of Edward. Hmm, ain't no telling wassup wit Walter. Scary ass white boy probably pissed his pants when he saw 'em."

The crew laughed and continued to discuss matters as DA drove away from the metal graveyard headed back to the city.

COP KILLAS II, RENEWED JUSTICE

Chapter 4

Ladies Night

This was the day the ladies, Dana and Sharon planned to go out on a shopping spree. Sharon wanted to go to the Beverly Center but Dana protested hard against the move. Dana complained about the atmosphere.

"I don't see how you do it Sharon," Dana said, slurping her drink from her straw. "Hanging around all those snobbish ass, racist white people. I'd be ready to pull a Nat Turner or Denmark Vesey on dat' ass."

"Guuurl please. Don't think I don't have my moments," Sharon confided. "Sometimes I be close girl to going in that weapons room, come back and kill every one of them racist ass pervs. Just throw a bang grenade and go in shooting."

"Ain't that how they train y'all?" Dana asked, rhetorically. "Shoot first and ask questions later."

"No. We're trained to shoot first," Sharon objected. "Then lie, frame you and then cover it up. Now that's correct police procedure."

The two women laughed as they strolled along the corridor window shopping.

"O' shit! We havta' go in here girl," Sharon spoke, abruptly detouring Dana by way of arm snatch. "They having a sale on Michael Kors purses."

Sharon dragged Dana inside the store so quick, Dana didn't get to sputter a word of disagreement. Dana was standing next to a display of purses before she could clear her throat.

"Damn Sis! All this for a purse?" Dana questioned. "You know that cracka didn't make his clothes for black women and he wish y'all stop sportin' his shit."

"What!" Sharon inquired, cynically staring at Dana as if she was waiting for Dana to admit she was just playing. "Girl I'm just buying a damn purse and with the right heels imma look fly."

"Sis, how long you been supporting the KKK?" Dana asked.

"Girl you know damn well I don't support no klans," Sharon barked, being slightly offended at the insinuation.

"O' yes you do my sister. Michael Kors, Tommy Hilfiger and a bunch of other crackas. You supporting all them klans from what I see," Dana finished, holding up quote fingers while she gave Sharon's outfit the once over.

COP KILLAS II, RENEWED JUSTICE

"What!" Sharon yelled, in disbelief. She took a moment glancing down at her own attire. She was embarrassed to admit it. She was wearing the clothing of three known racist. "Girl I'm glad you saved me from giving any more of my money to a racist. I won't be supporting the klan, any longer."

"I know that's right," Dana agreed, laughing and giving Sharon a fist up. "Black Power!"

"Yo' rap sheet didn't say anything about you being a militant," Sharon chuckled.

"I'm not a militant by a long shot but I won't knowingly be a sellout either," Dana emphasized. "Too bad some of these other sisters don't feel that way. They love making those racist fucks rich."

"Don't be so hard on 'em Dana," Sharon advised, giving her own sinister laugh. "Shit I just learned all this a minute ago. You have to give 'em time and besides some of these sisters really think this European shit makes 'em look good. I know I felt that way. Let's not get angry with the sisters and brothers who haven't gotten the memo yet."

"Look at this shit!" Dana yelled, losing her smile from Sharon's last comment. "Twenty five hundred for this bullshit purse. I don't think so."

"Excuse me ma'am, but we ask that you do not touch any of the displays unless you intend to buy it," A store clerk whispered, appearing behind the two women. "These are very expensive items and we don't want any accidental damage to occur."

"Hold up bitch! You think I can't afford this whack ass shit!" Dana screamed, dropping her soda to the floor and letting it splash. "Bitch! I'll buy yo' monkey ass and any of this euro trash in here, fucking retard."

"Chill out Dana," Sharon tried suggesting.

"Naw fuck this bitch!" Dana continued. "She looking like she wanna test my hands. Bitch wassup?"

The white woman quickly looked Dana up and down, twisting her lips in disapproval.

"I'm just conveying store policy ma'am," the woman answered. "Like I said a moment ago, if you can't afford it, please don't touch it ma'am. Thank you."

Dana pulled a bank roll of hundreds dollar bills from her pocket and ordered the lady to ring up three of the purses.

"Yeah hurry up and getcho' sorry ass to the counter bitch!" Dana ordered, following behind.

The white lady became very apologetic as she scurried back behind the counter to the register.

Dana stood mean mugging the woman as she calculated the total for the purses.

"That's going to be $7806 dollars and 11 cents," the woman said, staring at the large sum of money Dana was holding in her hand.

"Ok," Dana replied, counting off the bills. "Can you do me a favor hun?"

"Yes ma'am," The clerk answered.

"Can you dig that total outta yo' ass? Cause' I ain't buying shit from you, punk ass cave bitch," Dana yelled. "Tell yo' racist ass boss that you fucked that off!"

Dana and Sharon both laughed as they turned and walked out of the store. They discussed knowing the white lady was prejudice, and she only changed her attitude at the sight of dead green presidents.

"That's the very reason some blacks figure an economic boycott would teach these devils," Sharon offered. "They'll overlook race for a green dollar in a heartbeat."

"DA says economic boycotts will never force the cracka to equalize this nation or drop white supremacy. And what good is it if they continue to make their own money? We withhold a billion dollars from their economy and they print a trillion and put in circulation. We save a trillion dollars and build our own communities; they burn it down like they did Black Wall Street. I think most are trying to avoid that physical revolution or civil war this government and the racists are pushing for," Dana finished.

"For a hood girl you sure know how to use those big words," Sharon exclaimed, flashing the brightest smile.

"Girl I was a scholar throughout my school years," Dana replied. "You better ask somebody." The ladies continued to walk and laugh as DA's words captured their thoughts.

Both ladies were ready to eat now but Dana refused to spend another moment in uppity Beverly Hills, it was entirely too many crackas in that rich white city for Dana. They settled for a more diverse place, Inglewood.

The sun was going down early as the two sat outside the restaurant eating and looking along Market Street. The evening traffic was buzzing along Market Street and the pedestrians mimicked a small parade, everyone hustled along.

"Damn! You would think Inglewood was having a major event tonight or something," Sharon uttered, studying those passing by.

"I think we see…black people," Dana said, smiling from ear to ear.

Sharon joined in the hysterical laughter rolling herself around in her seat until something strange caught her attention. It changed her facial expression just long enough for Dana to see. Sharon dismissed the thought from her head and continued in the festive moment that she and Dana were enjoying.

"Girl what happened to you?" Dana asked, staring Sharon in the eyes. "You looked like you saw a ghost a minute ago."

"I'm good girl. Just thought I saw somebody," Sharon answered, as she continued to scan the opposite side of the street.

Sharon's phone ringing broke her stare. She looked down at the caller ID and pushed the accept call button.

"Hey Elliot," Sharon answered. "What's the word?"

Elliot's voice conveyed desperation as he urged Sharon to meet him in private as soon as possible.

"Twenty five minutes," Sharon spoke, pushing the end button on her phone and placing it back in its holster. "Dana we have to roll."

"What's the rush?" Dana inquired, following Sharon in a hurry, back to the new mustang DA gave her as a gift.

"I don't have time to drop you off so you gon' havta' roll with me," Sharon declared, looking intensely bothered by the call. "You armed Dana?"

"I'm always strapped," Dana replied, with her body springing forward from Sharon's thrust of the transmission in reverse. "Damn girl don't kill me fo' we get there."

Buckle up sistah," Sharon warned, slamming the shifter into the drive position. "I'm about to break this engine in right here, today girl."

Sharon's mustang flew down to Manchester Avenue and made a right turn headed for the 405 freeway on ramp.

Elliot was one of five other black cops that Sharon attended police academy training with. They all learned and suffered the stinging effects of those who practiced "Racism with a Badge."

One officer named Albert Harrison had finally succumb to the pressures of the dark side. He was selected "dick holder" for the racist white boys who could advance his career. He had left Sharon's clique over two years ago and been lewd to her since that day.

Officer Harrison once whispered a plan of rape in Sharon's ear to the cheers and applause of his crew; Sharon tried to attack him and had to be restrained by other officers. She remembered how happy he looked, like a puppy receiving a treat from his masters as they patted his bald head when he returned to his circle of cowardly misfits. She reported it and was placed on temporary leave of absence for reciting and instigating unfounded allegations against a fellow officer.

Sharon was nervous after the incident, she was harassed and threatened every day after she filed her report.

The other four officers, Belinda, Elliot, Ronald, and Mike took shifts watching over Sharon, rotating their nights to sleep over at Sharon's house as extra protection. It took Sharon many nights before she was able to find a good night's rest.

Sharon reiterated her experiences to Dana as she maneuvered the mustang in and out of lanes. Dana wondered why Sharon had stuck around for as long as she did.

"Where we headed?" Dana questioned.

"Downtown," Sharon replied. "The Alley."

"The Alley?" Dana repeated, dumbfounded. "Must be a helluva sale there, the way you driving."

"A friend of mines has some information and he sounded really nervous over the phone," Sharon revealed. "I think he's found something big on our commission or the police league."

"What's up with the alley though?" Dana asked, still blinded as to why Sharon was headed to downtown's fashion district.

"It's always crowded and easy to lose someone one following you," Sharon divulged. "Plus the noise of the crowd makes it difficult for anyone to mic up or record your conversation with all that fancy spy equipment. These devils use every trick or tool they can."

"That much I do know," Dana agreed.

Sharon talked more about her crew and Dana listened while they rode along, the downtown skyline was visible now.

Dana posed the question she had thought about earlier in her head and Sharon took a deep breath. Sharon paused wondering was it worth it.

"At first I was trying to do something I thought was noble; admirable even," Sharon confessed. "You know, help rid the community of crime, be a positive role model for children growing up in the inner city. Hmm, did I ever learn the hard way! It's more criminals wearing badges and three piece suits than there are walking the streets of LA."

Sharon merged with the crowded downtown traffic pulling over on the corner.

"Why you stopping here?" Dana asked, looking around the busy street. "The Alley across the light in the middle of the block."

"You getting out here. Hang around this end of The Alley. Act like a regular shopper just browsing or something," Sharon directed. "You'll see me and Elliot walk right pass you, if you see anyone following us call my phone. Let it ring but don't hold it up to your ear, put it in your pocket. If we being followed, make your way home."

"Got you," Dana replied, giving her weapons a last minute inspection before tucking them in her waist band and exiting the vehicle.

Dana began her stroll towards the alley as Sharon accelerated away. Dana stopped at one of the many refreshment booths along The Alley. She ordered a drink since she lost the last one earlier in a temporary moment of rage.

Dana hadn't been down here in years, and not much outside of the merchandise being sold had changed. She frolicked along the different vendors pretending to be a potential customer as she moved along.

Dana had neared the middle portion of The Alley when she spotted Sharon and Elliot moving in her direction. She walked into a booth and began to inquire about a grey and black Khaki jacket; Dana was into some men's attire.

The man grabbed his long metal hook and pulled the jacket down while Dana watched Sharon and Elliot passed in deep discussion. The man passed Dana the jacket and Dana held it up to her eye level.

"Forty five dollars," the man uttered, as Dana stood with her back to him; glaring outside.

She spread the jacket wide while turning it from front to back, as she continued to scan the largely packed crowd moving along.

Dana's mind was just about to call off the search when she noticed two men traveling along both sides of The Alley. The white man nearest her sported a cap and dark glasses; he kept his hand to his ear. Dana spotted the clear plastic coil like wire connected to his ear. She could smell a pig.

Dana put the jacket on, grabbed a baseball cap from the shelf and pulled a hundred dollar bill from her money and gave it to the man. The man said he would return with her change; Dana instructed the man to keep it as she moved back towards the entrance of the booth.

Dana stopped short eyeing a display glass.

"How much for the blade?" Dana asked.

The man reached in the display case, grabbed the blade and handed it to Dana.

"You've already paid young lady," the man returned.

Dana stood in the threshold of the booth glaring over the crowd behind the two men, no one else looked suspicious. Dana walked out of the booth and followed the crowd keeping her eyes on the two men, she was certain were tailing Sharon and Elliot.

~

Sharon and Elliot walked the crowded corridor as they talked.

"The Commission was made of up of some dirty politicians stealing every dime they could get their hands on, but the police league was and still is a completely corrupt entity," Elliot shared. "In fact there's a rumor that says unless you're willing to kill one of your own, you can't be brought in. No member has truly ever joined, their all selected. Hand-picked mercenaries."

"Just like the detectives that were killed," Sharon added.

"Uh-huh. It seems somewhere in the 1990's the Commission and the Police League had a big falling out. Even though the Commission was supposed to be the authority of the two, the Police League exercised full control," Elliot told. "The big wigs of the Police League blatantly bullied and intimidated members of the Commission. In two separate incidents, two commission members were found dead; both cases were labeled suicide by the coroner. No one was ever brought to justice or questioned."

"Mercenaries and assassins," Sharon interjected. "You can only wonder how many people they've got away with killing."

COP KILLAS II, RENEWED JUSTICE

"According to some of the old reports I've read, the number was high as thirty," Elliot continued, passing a small file over to Sharon. "Anybody who spoke a word against this group came up dead. These fuckas were suspected of killing several rich business men, drug dealers and every witness willing to testify against them. Hell they were even suspected of killing a doctor, a judge and a pair of prominent black attorneys who were investigating damn near everybody within LAPD's top brass. Not one grand jury indictment though."

Sharon understood the implications quite well. The police league ruled with an iron fist and a bloody sword.

"With that kinda' shit going on," Sharon started, pausing a second to process the information. "They were bound to have people in high places under their thumb."

"Exactly! The then coroner and mayor for certain," Elliot assured, catching something suspect in a mirror hanging from a booth's entrance way. "And I'm pretty sure it was more than just them two feeling the pressure."

Elliot was dropping mental bombs on Sharon when his gut started sending signals.

D. MANN

"Hey let's stop at that taco cart and grab something to eat," Elliot urged, dragging Sharon by the elbow. "Don't look! We gotta tail. Two white boys. The first one twenty five feet away; the second about forty feet, both to our six o'clock."

Sharon spotted Dana about fifty feet back and checked her phone for a possible missed call; nothing. She took the moment her phone turned black to use it as a mirror. She made the two white boys in caps lingering around their areas.

"Why exactly the tail?" Sharon questioned.

"Somebody went in the Archives room at Parker Center and removed all the files pertaining to the police league and commission," Elliot continued, changing his position to keep the two men in sight.

"Cover up," Sharon guessed.

"Yeah, but the commander came back on Ronald's shift asking about missing files," Elliot said, indicating the first source of their current predicament. "Ronald got to the files right before the files came up missing from the Archives room. But he only copied them. Somebody else stole 'em."

"They suspect Ronald?" Sharon asked, rhetorically.

Elliot nodded his head.

"Ronald told me other day his locker and his home were ransacked," Elliot informed. "And his superior has been riding his back for everything since that day; he finally put in for a transfer."

Elliot paid the owner of the stand and took another glanced at their followers, they were still hanging back. He and Sharon continued walking as they ate and talked.

"I've been seeing a tail on me for nearly the past 48 hours," Elliot notified. "I just moved my family to Arizona three days ago until this blows over and my house was broke into last night."

"Where are the copies of the files now?" Sharon asked.

"Housekeeping," Elliot replied.

"Why there?" Sharon questioned, quizzically.

"Didn't know where else to take 'em," Elliot answered. "Shit has really turned up a notch since someone started asking the right questions."

"Let's chill here for a second," Sharon suggested, pulling her phone and holding it up as if she was trying to get a signal. "Check our view."

Elliot pretended to look at shirts while Sharon studied her phone. She still hadn't received a call from Dana.

They both witnessed one of their followers take a seat attempting to hide his presence. A few minutes later the other follower took a seat concealing himself with the large moving crowd.

"They're trying to hide," Sharon spoke.

"Yeah I see that," Elliot responded. "C'mon, let's keep it moving while they play possum."

"So who's still around from the hay days?" Sharon probed.

"A lot of the people mentioned in the files that I've read so far are still alive," Elliot assured.

"So what part did the chief play in all this?" Sharon requested.

"Don't know," Elliot confided. "He was just a low level league member at that time."

"Nevertheless he was a league member," Sharon countered. "A chosen member. I'm gon' to need to get a look at those files."

"Help yourself. You know where they're at," Elliot returned. "Just make sure you're not being followed."

"Speaking of which I haven't seen our stalkers in a minute," Sharon said, now scoping out the area. "You?"

"Naw," Elliot commented. "Haven't seen 'em since they started playing hide-go-seek. Maybe they got pulled off surveillance detail."

"Possible. Thanks for everything Elliot," Sharon said, giving Elliot a hug. "Be careful and watch your back."

"You too," Elliot returned.

~

Dana walked out of the booth calm, cool and collected placing her cap on her head. She made her way through the crowd moving along the outer edges of it. She could hear Pocket's voice in her head guiding her steps.

Dana walked up behind the first man grabbing his shoulder. The man turned around and Dana buried the man's face into her neck silencing any loud noise. She leaned in closely to him, pushed her blade with force upwards while twisting into the man's sternum.

D. MANN

Cover the mouth, lean in, push up hard, twist and they'll lay themselves across your shoulder like a baby, nice and quietly. Dana could hear Pockets' words as she followed his instructions. It worked!

It was just as Pocket's had told her; the man buckled without making a sound. The man held both his hands across his stomach as he sat down. Dana pulled his cap down over his eyes and searched his pockets for identification. She found it, put it in her pocket and blended back into the crowd.

Dana spotted the other man on the opposite side of the walkway. He seemed to be having some communication problems, as he continually finger tapped the coiled plastic wire connected to his ear. The man seemed befuddled; staring at Sharon and Elliot, then looking cross the way behind himself.

The man was obviously confused, looking for his partner who he had lost communication with. Dana could sense his dilemma and continued to follow the dead man's partner. The partner must have assumed it was some technical problem because he stayed on his assignment.

Dana saw the perfect upcoming spot to neutralize her next victim; she sped her pace. Dana didn't have to worry as long as the man couldn't yell; no one would pay them any attention. Downtown Los

COP KILLAS II, RENEWED JUSTICE

Angeles was littered with homeless men and women whose bed was a concrete sidewalk. Another stretched out body in downtown Los Angeles wouldn't raise a hair.

She was now closing in on the second man, her heart pounded a little heavier this time as she neared his back side. With another touch on the shoulder the man turned around into gut wrenching pain. Dana muffled any possible sound the man could have made by smashing his face against her neck.

The man's scream was never heard as Dana applied extra force in her push upwards, twisting into his sternum. He fell over Dana's shoulder gently; Dana laid the man down next to a toy display and searched his body. She found what she was looking for and kept it moving.

~

Sharon hustled back to her car only to find Dana leaning against it sucking down a smoothie.

"What you doing here?" Sharon asked, making her way around to the driver's side of her car. "I thought I told you to make your way home if I was being followed. I know you saw the two guys behind us."

"I saw them," Dana responded. "The problem was they didn't see me. I handled both of their asses with ease, like two babies."

"Whatchu' mean handled?" Sharon inquired, closing her car door and glancing over at Dana.

"Handled dem' fools," Dana shot back, closing her door. "Took dey' ass down; you know killed dey' ass off."

"Girl stop playing," Sharon hissed.

"I'm bout' as serious as death and taxes," Dana answered, tossing Sharon the two identifications she had snagged from the bodies. "Still think I'm playing."

Sharon took a moment to investigate the ID's, neither brought any remembrance or stated an occupation. The two cards were basic California identification cards. Sharon would run them through the cop's database later.

Sharon fired up the engine and headed for the exit. As soon as she turned out, she and Dana noticed two squad cars pulling in with wailing lights.

"That was just in time. Somebody musta' found our sleepers," Dana alerted.

"Damn good timing. They'll be locking this place down in a little," Sharon warned, as she joined the multitudes of cars in the crowded downtown traffic.

She was on her way to share the information with the rest of the crew. She was about to put Dana up on game now.

Chapter 5

The Alliance

"Bruh, with all this new shit happening," Crafty spoke, climbing out of his truck to an awaiting DA. "I think it's about time to bring in some help. We got dudes following us around, taking shots at us n-shit. I'm starting to feel like shit about to hit the fan."

"We need somebody computer savvy and I'm definitely thinking about bringing in some skilled help," DA spoke. "It's time."

"I agree. I agree," Pockets chimed in, closing his car door and joining in the forming discussion. "I gotta' few killas who'll get down just on the strength of fuck the police. But I gotta' special homeboy for this mission. I'm finna' round my crew up. You cool witdat' DA? You cool witdat'?"

"If it's your crew Pockets, hell yeah I'm cool wit' it," DA settled, glancing over to Crafty who expected some challenge from DA. "I don't even know the brothers. But if they fucking with Pockets I'm sure about two things. One, they ain't snitching and two, they ain't gun shy. Might be the edge we need."

"I think we should bring in the Bag Brothers," Crafty advised. "It'd be nice to have their skills on hand if the funk pops off."

"Yeah I've been thinking the same thing. Skilled help," DA admitted, grabbing two shoulders of supplies from his truck and following Dana and Sharon inside the building. "Grab the rest of that shit and C'mon."

Crafty and Pockets grabbed the duffle bags from the rear of the truck and hustled inside behind the crew.

The crew gathered in the kitchen. Most were on their phones rounding up additional crew members while they briefly discussed their latest discoveries.

The men showed signs of success as they no longer spoke on their phones and unloaded the bags of its equipment.

"Where you say we havta' go to get the rest of those files?" DA questioned, Sharon.

"Out to Hemet," Sharon replied. "My people have it and they'll meet us there."

"I already got shit prepared for them so I hope they down with our game plan," DA spoke, with a tone of threat to it.

The entire room became silent as DA issued what most took as a one-time warning.

"My people might have to kill several cops just to survive the work day," Sharon argued. "I'll say they're more than down."

The crew looked at each other and nodded.

"Damn why so far out? Hemet out in the desert," Crafty asked, smiling and breaking the intense moment. "Cops can't hide shit in the hood no more?"

"Hell naw," Sharon retorted. "Never hide cheese around rats."

With the increase of violence the crew was beginning to experience, everyone was now gifted a black jumpsuit with woven Dupont Kevlar. A lightweight bullet proof vest was added for extra protection. DA highly recommended the crew get used to wearing them constantly.

"Aww shit!" Pockets exclaimed. "Bruh dun blessed us with some OO7 type shit. I'm putting in work. I'm putting in work."

"So what kind of information you have in that file you brought?" DA asked, smiling at Pockets as Pockets turned the jumpsuit from front to back.

"Don't know exactly," Sharon answered, opening the file and taking a glance. "We'll know in a little bit though."

"This is tight DA," Crafty spoke, studying the jumpsuit. "You can feel light plating in the backside too."

"A little sumthin' extra to watch your back," DA returned, focusing on a duffle bag laid against his chair.

The crew took to their individual tasks unpacking. Sharon sat down and read in disbelief.

"Most of this is pretty much common knowledge now but we have a couple names we can research," Sharon added, still perusing the file. "We need to find out if the coroner and mayor from back then are still alive."

"Yeah that's cool but are we exactly sure who in this group is being followed," DA inquired. "The first time we believe they were following Sharon. The second time they were on stakeout at Jonah's and the third time they were following Elliot."

"I believe it's an internal thing on my end. My brothers and sisters are under the scrutiny of the department," Sharon commented. "Somebody high up is looking to clean up some old dirt real fast."

"You sure your people gon' meet us there?" DA asked.

"Yeah they'll be there when we arrive," Sharon confided.

"I called up the Bag Brothers to see if they wanted to lend a hand," DA stated. "They accepted."

"I like dem' dudes right there," Pockets spoke, showing excitement. "Nigga dem' muthafuckas legendary. I studied all their shit! They got some of the greatest kills in Compton, LA and Watts. Dem' brothers da' shit and you know they witdat' Black movement."

"Yeah I heard the rumor they started as BGF (Black Guerilla Family) back in the days," Crafty inputted. "Say they were some of the coldest killers walking the earth."

"Why they call themselves the Bag brothers though?" Dana questioned.

"Besides it being their government names, it was said that if you had the misfortune of meeting those two, you better have a bag of money or you'd be getting the bag of death," Sharon answered. "They're legendary. We studied their profiles at the academy. They're the poster children for crazed, psychotic killers. They even terrified the shit out of the cops and never had one conviction against them. Rumor has it that they once kidnapped an officer from the inside of a Police station."

"Damn they were some cold dudes back then," Pockets roared.

"DA, how you meet 'em?" Dana questioned, again.

"Shiiid! I had a bag of money for 'em," DA uttered, with a smile to the laughs of the group. "They wasn't hitting me witda' bag of death."

The group's humor continued until individual work took over again. It looked like the crew were preparing for a small war of some sort. DA interrupted the quietness to begin syncing their two way radios and watches.

"Dis' some nice hardware right here," Crafty said, gripping the AR-15 rifle and checking his sights.

"Yeah Pockets came through on that one," DA spoke, giving his approval while he inspected some of the twin Glock pistols Pockets provided.

"My baby connected," Dana interjected, proudly.

"So we see," DA returned, smiling and checking his own weapon.

"The Asians got everything. It's good to have few homies from China Town," Pockets shared, adjusting the rifle's stock. "Man this bitch sweet. I'm red dotting foreheads."

The crew began loading the various weapons and extra clips, they weren't going to be out gunned again nor caught off surprise. They spent the next few hours preparing themselves for any battle.

"When we take off to go get those files I wanna stop and pick up my girl B," Crafty stated.

"You wanna bring Bearilla in?" DA sounded off.

"You wanna tell her no?" Crafty shot back.

DA thought about it quickly.

"I guess she rollin' then," DA agreed. "But note how serious this shit is getting bruh, deadly."

"She'll have me and her uncles to watch over her," Crafty alerted, with a bright smile.

"Her uncles? Who the Bag Brothers?" Pockets questioned, in confusion.

"Oh snap! That's who she be talking about," Dana blurted out. "She said she had some uncle's wit' the business."

"Yeah. B is the Bag Brother's niece," Crafty admitted.

"That's my girl. And that big ass broad don't fuck around," Dana warned. "I saw her get off witda' Desert Eagle like it was .22 revolver and she still the only woman I ever saw break a man's jaw with one hit."

"Yeah my lady a beast," Crafty added, blushing from his proud moment. "That's why I need her rolling shotgun with me. She got my back."

"I don't know if we have a vest big enough for Bearilla," DA uttered, in a low tone.

"I heard that shit DA!" Crafty alerted, quickly with a stare to match.

"Just make sure you gotta' vest and a two way radio for her," DA advised, zipping his bags closed. "Hopefully one of those suits fit her big ass."

"I already got her synced up," Crafty informed. "And she can fit a suit my size ol' busta…with yo' stressing ass."

"Then let's get ready to roll out," DA instructed, grabbing his equipment bag and making his way to the back door. "We can snatch up yo' girl first then go get the Bag Brothers. Pockets what's up with your crew?"

"They meeting us here. They should be pulling up any minute," Pockets' answered. "I told 'em to pack up the big shit."

"Cool," DA replied.

The crew cleaned and packed up. They carried their bags outside to the new vehicles awaiting them out back.

The group gave a last minute inspection of one another before loading up in the three new Chevy Suburban's, DA had specially ordered, modified and reinforced, waiting out back.

"Man these trucks are nice bruh," Crafty spoke.

"Bullet proof windows, armor siding and puncture proof tires. We rolling in mini tanks from here on out," DA acknowledged. "Shit, what's the use in having money if you can't use it when you really need it."

Pockets' phone begin ringing. He pushed the talk button icon.

"We in the back," Pockets spoke, into the phone before pushing the end button icon. "My people here."

Pockets stood on the side of the building directing his crew towards him.

COP KILLAS II, RENEWED JUSTICE

"Everybody this is Bloodstone, Fingers, Mayhem and Brazy," Pockets' offered. "Brazy the one with that special gift DA."

Dana was first to greet the quartet, she had already known them since middle school. The rest of the crew welcomed the quartet for the first time.

The four men looked like throwbacks from the movie *Colors*. It was easy to recognize that Fingers and Mayhem were Crips, and Bloodstone and Brazy were definitely Blood gang members, their fat red shoe laces were as bright as a stop sign.

Pockets ushered the men to the back of the truck he was driving and ordered them to throw their bags in the back.

The crew swapped their vehicles for the suburban's parking spots in the back and took off for their next destination.

It took nearly an hour before the convoy of trucks arrived at Bearilla's address. The group watched in silence as she made her appearance.

"Those steps sound like they're screaming for help," Pockets whispered, with an ear to ear smile on his face as Bearilla descended the front porch.

D. MANN

With every step she took downwards Pockets voice could be heard squeaking. Help! Help! Help!

Dana and the four men couldn't save themselves from immediate laughter.

"Leave my home girl alone fa' she whoop yo' ass," Dana demanded, through near tears.

"Shiiid! I ain't fighting her," Pockets admitted. "I'll put a shell in her big-o-ass though. What she weigh? Every bit of two moons and a planet. Got me fucked up you think I'm taking an ass whooping from her. That's too much of an embarrassment; too much of an embarrassment."

"Don't be scared blood. You just can't let her fall on you," Brazy added, causing the entire truck occupancy to fall in deep but quiet laughter.

"Oh my lord," Sharon whispered, at the sight of Bearilla.

"Yeah she a big one ain't she," DA muttered, rhetorically while laughing under his breath.

"Oooooh big ain't the word baby," Sharon responded, in awe. "How did she get through that door? Who makes her clothes?"

Bearilla waved to DA, Dana and Pockets as she headed towards the truck Crafty was driving.

COP KILLAS II, RENEWED JUSTICE

Bearilla approached Crafty kissing his puckered lips, as he leaned out of his driver's side window.

"Hey baby," Crafty announced, smiling.

"Don't hey me! You was supposed to pick me up last night," Bearilla scolded, quickly changing her mood as she walked around to the passenger's side. "I'd be wrong if I flipped yo' truck over and started a rumble huh? I can hear you crying right now, why you starting with me girl?"

"Naw. I would be crying about why yo' ass so deaf though," Crafty retorted, giving Bearilla his that's a shame face, while she closed the door and squirmed around getting comfortable. "How you forget that fast when I just told you last night? I told you I was busy and wouldn't see you until today."

"I love you Mr. Crafty," Bearilla stated, with another change of mood. "I was just missing my Boo-Boo."

"Well yo' Boo-Boo was missing his Bear too," Crafty confided, leaning over to kiss Bearilla.

Honk! Honk! Honkkk!

"Can we get a move on it or must we watch this episode of love and hamburgers!" DA yelled, urging the loving couple parked in front of them.

"I see DA bleeding again," Bearilla spoke, flashing DA a fuck you finger out the window. "Yo' homeboy stay on his period."

"Yeah I love you too like steak and eggs," DA returned, yelling out of his window again. "Now can we roll please? Thank you."

"Ooh he such a smart ass," Bearilla commented, strapping her seat belt across herself. "I should flip his truck over." Click! "Damn this seat belt tight!"

The convoy was on its way again to DA's liking. The Bag Brothers were thirty minutes away and DA was anxious to learn more.

Everyone in the crew was surprised when the address they pulled up to, to pick up the Bag Brothers was less than a hundred feet away from a local police station.

"Is this the right address?" Crafty asked, looking confused.

"I have no idea. I see my uncles when they show up at my house," Bearilla answered, confused herself.

DA, Dana, Pockets and Sharon all wondered the same question. *Is this the right address?*

COP KILLAS II, RENEWED JUSTICE

Everyone received their answer when the brothers emerged from their dwelling with one duffle bag apiece.

The brothers nearly favored twins their looks were so identical. The only visible difference was one was clearly taller than the other. They wore all black military style attire, boots, gloves, and long overcoats. Both sported afros capped by black Derby's.

Their appearance seemed youthful for the age range of mid to late fifties, they looked as if they were in their early forties. It was obvious the two brothers were into working out, their physiques showed the signs of consistent exercise.

The smaller brother locked their door while the other stood nearly back to back with him, eyeing the block intensely. The smaller brother turned facing the convoy and with perfect synchronization the two marched down the stairs.

The brothers nodded their heads in acknowledgement of DA in their fast paced march to the backseat of Crafty's truck.

The taller brother opened the back door of Crafty's truck and climbed in. The shorter brother turned towards the house, pulled a cellular device from his pocket, pressed a button, and waited a second for the screen to flash before climbing in the backseat himself.

"Wassup Bear?" The taller brother asked, extending his hand to Bearilla's shoulder.

"How you doing Uncle Kid?" Bearilla responded, laying her hand atop of his.

"I'm good," Uncle Kid replied. "Wassup witchu' Crafty?"

"Just maintaining Unc," Crafty told.

The shorter brother closed the door and repeated the question. "Wassup Bear?"

"Wassup Uncle Nap? How you doing? I haven't seen y'all in about a year," Bearilla interrogated, being jerked backwards in her seat as Crafty pulled away from the curb."

"Shit I'm good," Uncle Nap informed. "We been staying under the radar doing our thing, keeping current you know? What about y'all? What you and Crafty been up to lately?"

"I ain't been up to shit," Bearilla answered. "But Crafty been playing spy games lately. Everything so hush-hush and covert nowadays, I feel like I'm sleeping with a CIA agent."

COP KILLAS II, RENEWED JUSTICE

"Well you damn sure about to get briefed today because shit is way crazy," Crafty cut back in, getting ready to catch the brothers and Bearilla up to speed on the events of late.

Crafty told the brothers and Bearilla as much as he knew about the impending mission as they now followed DA and Sharon along the freeways.

~

The crew arrived at what appeared to be some abandoned mass factories. There were several huge run down structures that created a maze of the entrance and grounds. There were twelve buildings in total, erected in groups of three.

The structures were connected by second and third story bridges that ran along the inside and outside track of the buildings. Each group of three buildings were called complex 1 through 4. Complex 2 was commonly referred to as the Central Factory.

DA was directed to the back of the Central Factory by Sharon where blew the horn. A large bay door opened and the crew pulled into the warehouse section of the factory.

Belinda, Mike, Ronald and Elliot stood ready to greet the group as they exited their trucks.

Sharon made the quick introductions and ushered the group to follow while she toured the group around the factory.

The central factory housed several resting rooms on the third floor, as well as two full size kitchens on the first floor and numerous bathrooms on all three levels of the edifice. The crew would sleep in the central factory.

"This facility used to house one of the best video monitoring systems money could buy," Belinda shared. "We've been able to get most perimeter cameras back online and most of the inner cameras were already working. We just had to jumpstart the system and now we can watch it all from second floor monitoring room."

"Only bathrooms and resting rooms have no video surveillance," Mike interjected. "For the most part, once we got the power running our sight was virtually everywhere. As long as no one was followed, I think we'll all be safe here."

The group chose the second floor's enormous break room as its strategic war room. It had a movie screen that deployed from the ceiling.

DA was ready to conference.

COP KILLAS II, RENEWED JUSTICE

Most chose to situate themselves before conferencing, it was possible they would be spending a couple days or more at the factory if needed.

Sharon demanded everyone took the next few hours to get to know each other, they would be working closely with one another from here on out. Everyone there fully understood the purpose and consequences of this gathering.

The crew was shown the rest of the facility and took a break to unwind themselves. Some of the group rested in the break room and indulged in idle chatter. Mike grabbed his bags and began rummaging through his belongings. Brazy in his stroll pass Mike to the water fountain spied a shiny object in Mike's bag.

DA, Sharon, Crafty and Bearilla sat in one of the offices huddled up in discussion while the Bag brothers were in full stride with their rigorous workout routine when the sounds of an argument broke out in the break room.

DA and Sharon rushed in the break room to find Mike and Brazy being separated by Elliot as the rest of the group filed in the room out of curiosity.

"Dis muthafucka' a pig blood!" Brazy yelled, pointing over Elliot's shoulder into the face of

Mike. "Check his bag blood, nigga gotta' badge in dat muthafucka."

"Everybody just calm down," Sharon interrupted, attempting to take control of the growing feud.

"Fuck dat blood! Check his bag! Check his gotdamn bag!" Brazy continued, still pointing in Mike's face.

"You better move that finger boy before you lose it," Mike warned, slapping Brazy's hand and causing another brief skirmish to ensue.

The other men all moved in to separate Mike and Brazy whose fight had become a tussle.

"He must be cool cuzz if he fucking with Pockets," Mayhem added, secretly enjoying the sight of a slight tussle between the two men.

"Pockets you know dis' muthafucka a pig blood?" Brazy asked.

"Naw. But I know she is," Pockets answered, indicating Sharon. "And she fully witda' business and those her people, so chill out homie; it's all good. It's all good, we united in cause."

"Alright blood," Brazy agreed. "But I'm feeling kinda' muslim with all this pork in here."

COP KILLAS II, RENEWED JUSTICE

"I'm in agreement wit' cuzz on that one," Mayhem added, to the growing resentment. "They supposed to be working with us or running background checks on us? You know I ain't never been down with no cops cuzz."

The entire group began to argue until DA and Crafty started over yelling the group to regain control.

"Everyone here in this room is here for one thing and one thing only...Justice!" Crafty growled, glaring in the eyes of every man and woman present. "Let's understand this shit for what it is right now! We not here to make arrest," Crafty continued, glaring at the unknown officers. "We here to kill the guilty and only the guilty. We don't need ANY IDIOCY either! One dumb ass mistake can cause death for everyone here. Getcha' shit together. This is the team and this is our mission. Anybody got a problem witdat' speak now?"

Dana leaned over smiling and whispered in DA's ear, "There he go trying to speak intelligent again."

DA smiled.

"I got one question," Fingers spoke, eyeing the officers with intensity and a mindset of an early cop killing. "Any of y'all trying to make captain?"

Everyone focused on the officers who the question was posed to. Not one officer took it as an insult, just a desire to know.

"You don't have an idea of what we've been through. We just trying to make it alive another day son," Elliot answered.

"We we're all forced out on stress leave," Belinda answered, pulling her pistol and cocking it. "Effective immediately."

"Well since the fun and games are over now and everybody looks present and accounted for; let's get down to business," DA ordered, standing before his seat at the table. "One thing I want everyone here to know. You're here because I asked for your help, not to run shit. We clear?"

The group didn't say a word. They nodded their heads in agreement and began taking seats throughout the room. Sharon stood at the front with Ronald and began briefing the group on everything she knew the files stated. Ronald tossed a backpack on the table and started pulling items from the inside.

"Most of dudes that the files discuss are still alive and we've been able to find locations for most of them," Ronald confided, searching through one particular file. "This dude here is someone we definitely wanna talk too. His name is Steven White, he was one of the reporters from the LA Times who quickly and quietly backed off the investigation of the Police League. I'm sure he has something to tell us. He's a resident of Hollywood."

Ronald attached Steven's picture to a cork board and placed another white man's picture next to his.

"This guy here is John Whitecloud. A five dollar Indian," Ronald stated, before being interrupted.

"A five dollar Indian?" Fingers questioned, with the look of bewilderment across his face. "Fuck is that?"

"Back in the days after the cracka slaughtered the Indians, the United States government decided to pay reparations to the Indians for the crimes committed against them," DA told. "Most of the crackas got pissed when they heard about these reparations so the government allowed the crackas to put their names on a list that was solely intended for Indian reparations. The government charged the crackas five dollars and that sir is what the fuck a five dollar Indian is."

"Dirty muthafu…," Fingers yelled, before he was interrupted.

"And Mr. Whitecloud here is no different from the rest of 'em," Ronald spoke, taking back over the conversation. "Another conniving azz honkie. He was one of the longest tenured commission members during his reign, and that's exactly what it was; his reign. He was definitely one of the power wielding members. He was marked for having what the files quoted as *Heavy Influence*."

Ronald grabbed another picture from a folder and placed it on the corkboard next to John Whitecloud's.

"This she devil here," Ronald said, pointing at the picture of the white woman. "Her name is Susan Whitmore or as she was appropriately called back then, Susan Whoremore. It was said that her only true crime was sleeping with anyone breathing. She was queen of pillow talk, which most believe was the reason someone tried to Marilyn Monroe her. Also the reason we believe someone big went out their way to have her spared. Two hit men were found D.O.A in her home. She disappeared only to resurface for a grand jury indictment of a then Sergeant Dirk Holloway where she couldn't recall a thing."

"Sounds like somebody saved her from a hit," Pockets inputted. "The question is why?"

"She was a secret keeper," Kid Bags divulged, grabbing everyone's attention.

"Whatchu' mean," Bloodstone asked, perplexed about the statement. "The bitch be keeping niggas secrets?"

"Naw. I remember this case vividly," Kid Bags continued. "She was called the secret keeper because she had dirt on everybody...and I mean everybody. She knew who the dope heads and tri-sexuals were. She knew who liked little boys and girls. She had the dirt on everything from murders committed by crooked cops to every penny stolen by a banker. This broad had more power than a little. She was considered one of the most powerful devils in Los Angeles back then."

"It's all hearsay but they say she got a heads up on the hit and had her own welcoming committee greet those two amateurs," Nap Bags inserted. "It was never proven but it was believed that she personally poisoned the man who sponsored the hit on her life."

"Our files must have missed that part," Sharon said, giving a well done nod to the Bag brothers.

"Have any of you ran across the name Henry Robertson anywhere throughout your research?" Kid Bags inquired, searching everyone's face.

The Officers looked at each other to find no answer. They all shook their heads no. DA and the rest of their crew all looked around searching for a yes while shaking their own head's no. No one in the room was familiar with the name.

"He was a very rich business man with more than his hands and money deep into the commission," Nap bags taught. "They always teach you to follow the money…Henry Robertson was the money. He was the major contributing factor to the fall of the Commission and Police League even though the media ignored that entire connection."

"You said he was," Dana inserted. "Dude must of wound up dead too."

"Yeah he was mysteriously poisoned," Nap bags informed.

"Ahh! The bitch Susan," Mayhem guessed.

The Bag brothers nodded their approval.

"Makes a lot more sense now," Elliot blurted out, standing and pacing back and forth. "The large recorded amounts of money indicated in the Commission's legend that never had a source. John Whitecloud simply bought the Commission and now we know who his boss was."

"Not everyone was in his pocket," Ronald added, placing another three pictures on the board next to Susan's photo. "Meet Commission members Ellery Johnson, Ben Brooks and Gary Greyton III. The three most defiant and most threatened members of the Commission. All are still alive. Ben lives in Riverside, Ellery in Encino and Gary in Glendale. We should put a rush on making contact with these people. I think Ben, Ellery and Gary will be our best chance of finding out what the fuck is going on here. We should talk to them first."

"Just going around asking questions is only gon' raise suspicion about us so what's the plan for addressing Ben, Ellery and Gary?" DA asked.

"Belinda and Sharon can pose as reporters doing a piece on a current member of the Commission and redirect the questioning," Ronald proposed. "We can monitor them from a short distance away in case anymore mercenaries show up to ambush."

"Let's not forget the former mayor and coroner, especially the coroner," Dana reminded "He's hidden a whole bunch of shit."

"Oh he won't be forgiven," DA prompted. "Got something real nice planned for his ass."

The team continued to discuss the various measurements of their plans and every man and woman's individual duties. The time for reckoning was soon approaching.

COP KILLAS II, RENEWED JUSTICE

Chapter 6

House Cleaning

Sharon knocked on the door as her, Belinda and Crafty stood patiently waiting for an answer. Crafty held the Panasonic camera on his shoulder while he attempted to peek through the window.

"Even though her car is here it looks like she might be gone," Belinda whispered, to the group. "Imma check around the back."

Sharon nodded her head as she gave the doorbell another round of ringing. She spied through the window on her left side; she saw nothing. She was in motion to knock on the door again when it opened. Belinda greeted the unexpecting pair with an alarmed expression.

"Smells like foul play," Belinda informed, the pair as they stepped through the door.

Crafty placed the camera on the floor and drew his weapon from beneath his shirt. Sharon two-wayed their suspicions to the rest of the group while pulling her own pistol. The three began searching Ms. Ellery's house.

It wasn't long before the three searchers found the source of the odor. Ms. Ellery's body had been stretched out and bound by both her hands and feet. She was murdered in ritualistic fashion in her very own bed. The three covered their noses as they studied the grotesque scene.

"This look like some devil worshipping shit right here," Crafty acknowledged.

"Or a clever cover up," Sharon concluded, walking out of the bedroom. "Either way we just loss a potential lead."

The crew could here screeching tires out front, they knew it was the rest of their team about to make entrance.

Sharon appeared in the doorway as the rest of the team approached the front steps.

"She's D.O.A," Sharon informed, DA and Mike who were leading the pack. "And it appears to be too clean even for devil worshippers."

Mike entered the house followed by DA and the rest of the team. They entered the bedroom in awe noticing the many demonic drawings scrawled across the wall. Ms. Ellery laid tied to her bed post with carvings cut into her chest. The number 666 was cut into each of her exposed breast and her nipples were biting off.

"Sharon's right," Mike agreed, eyeing the deceased body. "It's way too clean for a cult killing. Somethings not right with this picture."

Mike began searching for clues while he canvassed the scene. The rest of the crew continued to look on in amazement

"Fuck it, we ain't got that kinda time to waste. Let's move on to Gary's," DA urged, making his way back out of the room.

The ten man squad left the house and loaded back into the two trucks with their destination set for Glendale. It wasn't a far distance away.

"Somebody staged that to appear as a cult killing y'all say huh?" DA inquired. "If so, why?"

"I don't know. It could just be random," Sharon responded. "But when it looks staged like that, it's almost impossible not to throw random out the window."

"Random has no place in this one," Mike uttered. "And at this point I have no more belief in coincidence."

"Coincidence never sat well with me either," Kid Bags joined in.

"Me neither," Nap Bags agreed.

D. MANN

The team rolled along for another fifteen minutes before they arrived at the Glendale address. The sun was just beginning to set when Belinda, Sharon and Crafty emerged from the vehicles.

Sharon approached the front door readying herself to knock, the door was already unlocked and partially left open. Sharon, Belinda and Crafty immediately pulled their weapons entering the premises. The rest of the crew noticed the trio pulled their weapons and quickly emerged from the vehicles themselves. They were right behind the trio as they entered.

The team discovered Gary in a small den in the back of the house. He was dead from one gunshot wound to the head. There was a note left on the table next to the chair Gary's body sat in indicating Gary had taken his own life. The entire team felt the suicide was bullshit.

"Somebody's cleaning house," DA shouted, having an epiphany.

"Then we better hurry it up and get to yo' boy Ben Brooks," Pockets exclaimed.

"Yeah! Cause old Ben on borrowed time," Fingers added.

"Gary hasn't been dead long either," Mike spoke, touching two fingers to Gary's neck. "His body still warm. Which means the killers can't be too far ahead of us."

The team rushed out the house and into the vehicles. They were speeding through traffic attempting to make up for any unknown time that may have been lost. Riverside was quite a distance away. It was possible they could beat the killers there.

"These muthafuckas must be operating off the same list we have," Crafty guessed.

"It's possible. We only have copies. Somebody else has the originals," Mike stated.

It took the team a little more than a hour to get to Ben's house. As soon as the team stepped out of the vehicles they could hear and see the exchange of gunfire through the upstairs windows.

"Breach the house!" Mike yelled, heading for the front door. "Take the back!"

Belinda, Crafty, Bearilla and Fingers quickly made their way to the back of the house. DA, Dana and Pockets joined Mike at the front door. Kid and Nap Bags used one another to scale the front of the house to make entrance through the bedroom window.

Blah! Blah! Blah! Blah! Blah! Blah! Blah! Ben's gun sounded off.

Ben was crouched down behind his dresser swapping in another clip when Kid and Nap Bags climbed through the window. Out of sheer nervousness Ben fumbled the gun attempting to point it at the Bag brothers.

"We're the good guys," Kid Bags told, firing his twin pistols towards the bedroom door and forcing a temporary retreat.

"Hurry up and get your pistol loaded and stay right on my hip," Nap Bags ordered.

"We got Ben!" Nap Bags screamed, into his two-way. "Coming down now!"

A barrage of shots began firing off. The shots seemed never ending to Ben as he could hear his home being decimated.

"We're pinned down! We're pinned down!" One of the assailants could be heard screaming.

The assailants were trapped outside of Ben's bedroom and the team were forcing their way up the stairs. Nap Bags motioned with his hands for Ben to stay put and with just a nod of their heads, the brothers sprang into action.

COP KILLAS II, RENEWED JUSTICE

Nap Bags began firing towards the top of the door while Kid Bags slid out in the hallway blazing all in sight.

The assailants were huddled near the corner of the hall desperately trying to stave off the mass attack coming from the bottom of the stairs. Kid Bags' aim found his targets as he slid against the rail. Nap Bags leapt out of the room with both his pistols exploding and Ben rushed out behind them firing his own pistol again. The guns of the three men chewed through the assailants bodies.

"It's all clear!" Nap Bags called out, glancing over the dead bodies of the assailants.

The rest of the team made their way to the top of the stairs where the brothers and Ben stood. Sharon and Mike started searching the bodies for identification or any clues to who they worked for.

"We're definitely gonna have to speed up our timetable," DA instructed. "Anybody who know anything has obviously been marked for death now."

"I agree," Mike conceded. We need to find those addresses for the rest of our targets before these jokers do."

"Nothing," Sharon exclaimed, finishing her search of the victims. Let's get Ben back to the compound. With this much gun fire I'm surprise the cops haven't arrived yet."

"Yeah let's get the fuck outta here," DA ordered. "Ben you're coming with us."

"Damn right I am!" Ben conceded. "Somebody just tried to kill me in my own home!"

The team rushed out of the house with Ben in tow and back into the trucks. They were being extra cautious to make sure they weren't being followed away from the scene.

"Somebody mind explaining to me please, why someone tried to have me murdered?" Ben asked, irritated and breathing extremely heavy. "Who you are? Why did you rescued me? And from the bottom of my heart; thank you guys. The sons of bitches would have killed me if you guys hadn't showed up when you did. Again," Ben continued, taking a deep breath and releasing a deep sigh. "Thank you."

"The pleasure was ours Ben," Kid bags said, with a slight smile and pat on the shoulder.

"My name is Sharon," Sharon spoke, taking over the conversation. "We believe you have information that could unveil the biggest criminal activity this city has ever seen."

"What information could I possibly have," Ben asked. "I spend my days quietly minding my own business. I'm a retiree."

"The information I'm referring to comes from more than twenty years ago sir," Sharon informed. "When you were a member of the Commission."

"Is that what this is all about?" Ben replied. "The Commission! They were a bunch of corrupt bastards but what does this have to do with now."

"Shortly before we arrived at your home we went to one of your ex-colleagues home. A Mr. Gary Greyton III," Sharon cited.

"Yeah Gary! He was actually one of the incorruptible members," Ben recalled, thinking back to the old days.

"We found him with a gunshot wound to the right side of his head and a phony suicide letter next to him," Sharon abreasted.

"What! Not Gary," Ben murmured, covering his mouth.

"Before we found Gary we found a Ms. Ellery Johnson. You don't even wanna know what condition we found her in," Sharon warned. "Someone or some group is trying to rid themselves of a past that's come back to haunt, and you guys seemed to be a critical piece to the puzzle."

Ben sat in the solitude of his mind for a moment. The new revelations came as a complete shock to him. Now he was simply processing the new information.

"How can I help y'all?" Ben voiced, seemingly resolved now.

COP KILLAS II, RENEWED JUSTICE

Chapter 7

Buncha' New Shit

"Anybody get the addresses on our coroner and mayor yet?" DA asked, walking into the break room.

"Sure did," Ronald replied, spinning away from his laptop. I found your coroner. He's a resident of Redlands, California. I'm having trouble locating the mayor because he became a governor at one time. I need a special clearance to access this database to get his current address."

"You can't go through the police database?" DA questioned, now standing at the coffee pot.

"Not without alerting them and giving away our position," Ronald returned. "That's why I'm trying to access this database here. They have one helluva security system, it's very complex."

"Let me have a look at that blood," Brazy asked, walking over to Ronald's laptop. "I'll bet money I can get in it."

Ronald rose from his chair and pushed it towards Brazy. "Be my guest. It can't hurt to give it a try but like I said, it's very complex. I've been working on this for over a hour now."

Brazy's fingers began tapping the keys like a professional typist. Within a couple of minutes of typing Brazy was announcing his victory.

"Here it is now," Brazy declared, spinning in the chair.

DA took note of the address.

"I'll be damned," Ronald murmured, staring at the laptop screen. How'd you do that? They have one of the most sophisticated systems on the market."

The rest of the team quickly gathered around the laptop in awe of Brazy's talent.

"Every security system has a back door to and through its firewalls blood," Brazy educated. "It's standard for the programmer to keep control. You just have to know it when you see dat shit."

"Where you learn that at?" Bearilla asked.

"In juvenile camp," Brazy answered. "While they we're teaching us how to create computer programs, this white boy who was locked up wit us taught some of us how to hack. He was using computers in a jailhouse class blood to steal tens of thousands from companies. Funny shit is, that's what he was in jail for in the first place."

"Talk about the system making criminals more advanced," Mike started. "Shit if you can learn that why you not working in Silicon Valley somewhere?"

"Blood wit a record like mines they ain't fucking wit me," Brazy answered.

Mike nor anyone else in the room could question the validity of Brazy's statement, everyone knew it was true. Once you had a criminal record, by law you were reinstated to slavery. Mike knew the 13th amendment well. Mike thought of the few black men that he had helped criminalize early in his career when he truly believed the system was fair and solely about getting justice for injustice. He had stop believing in those fantasies long ago. Mike thought to himself, *knowing what I know today I would have never arrested some of them brothers for the petty shit I booked them for*.

He witnessed first hand how racist the system was inside his very own department and how virtually every white officer was above the law.

"I don't think anyone here would have expected this from you," Ronald said, reclaiming the laptop momentarily. "But since you have those set of skills see if you can hack this site."

Brazy took over the laptop and had the site hacked in less than 30 seconds.

"You can do what you want with it now blood," Brazy instructed, raising from the chair. "It's wide open."

"Damn you got skills," Ronald acknowledged, giving Brazy's shoulder a stiff slap.

"Ben can you tell us something we may not know about the Commission and the Police League. A lot of good innocent people were killed fighting against their corruption," DA inquired, turning and walking over to Ben.

"I really don't know where to start," Ben said, pausing to think. "It was so much corruption; most of it was blatant."

"What can you tell us about Henry Robertson and his dealings with the Commission?"

"Nothing really new," Ben surmised. "Most of his dealings became public when he was found murdered. However, something that wasn't known about was that Henry had silent partners."

"Are you referring to Susan Whitmore?" Elliott spoke, joining in the questioning.

"Hell no!" Ben cursed, waving his arm. "She was just the bed wench for both men. One of Henry's silent partners was a ruthless dude by the name of Casey Kovac. He and Henry had an argument over

Susan and the shit hit the fan. They exhausted the business relationship and started publicly spilling secrets on each other. Short version of that story is Casey set off into the sunset with Susan but the damage was done."

"What damage?" DA asked, looking at the mayor's residence on the laptop.

"That whole fiasco set off a firestorm," Ben told. "It became public that some of the city officials, Commission members, Police League members and even the mayor were taking bribes from multi-million dollar companies for every illicit act you can imagine."

"People started feeling the heat?" Elliot figured.

"Man the heat was coming down and mouths were starting to run," Ben continued, receiving a cold bottle of water from Sharon. "Thank you. Once parts of the story came to life, it became a true scramble to save ass. The Grand Jury started passing out indictments like church bibles on an Easter Sunday. Name dropping was at an all-time high and then the bankers went to work."

"The bankers?" DA asked, curiously copying the mayor's address onto paper.

"Yeah. The bankers," Ben assured. "Once it became known that the Commission and the Police

League were sold to the highest bidder, the bankers went into clean up mode. Everything and everybody became an instant threat. To this day not one bankers's name was ever mentioned but all the leads started pointing in their direction."

"What kind of businesses were they funding?" Mike asked.

"Nothing ever on paper but they were behind the renovations at Hollywood Park Casino, numerous edifices built downtown, clubs, restaurants, you name it they had their money in it," Ben confided. "The bankers were even bank rolling the then, new Russian mob who were gaining prominence in the city at that time."

"Oh shit!" Ronald yelled, bringing a halt to the discussion being held. "Look at this y'all. We finally got a hit."

The crowd gathered around Ronald at the computer as the two faces pulled up on the screen.

"Those the two dudes I took down at The Alley," Dana blurted out.

"Correct you are my young sistah," Ronald agreed. "And both of your victims are confirmed ex-Police League members. Everybody meet deceased guy number one, Mark Stevenson and deceased guy number 2, Hank Kershaw. Both charged for a litany of shit but never convicted and both retired five years ago, and both receive full benefits. How fucking nice!"

"So now it's official," Crafty announced. "It's the Police League operating in mischief."

"Whose currently the head of the Police League?" DA asked.

"Ex-chief Darryl Fince," Belinda recalled, tapping her forehead.

"Darryl Fince!" Mike shouted. "Now that's a gotdamn shame! He's been through more investigations than Jesse Jackson."

"The league has been quiet in recent years," Belinda interjected.

"But for what reason though," Mike responded. "Because right now it looks like someone is still active."

"Okay y'all. Time for a change of plans," DA ordered, as the group made themselves comfortable settling in for further conversation.

Because of time restraints the group agreed to split in two teams. The Bag brothers, Crafty, Mayhem and Bearilla would kidnap the coroner and bring him back to the compound. DA, Dana,

Sharon, Pockets, Mike and Belinda would tend to the ex-mayor.

Because of the short distance between the mayor's and coroner's residence both teams felt comfortable being able to aid the other in short notice. The rest of the group would stay and guard the compound.

The teams suited up in preparation for the impending mission and wished each other luck as the two teams headed out.

Chapter 8

Highway of Hell

Nap Bags spied through the binoculars glaring over both levels of the house.

"He in there alone," Nap Bags told.

"Ok y'all stay here and cover our backs," Kid Bag ordered. "We going in to get him."

"Imma take position between the two cars in the driveway in case we spot a creeper," Mayhem added, sliding out of the vehicle behind the Bag brothers.

"This is so exciting," Bearilla whispered, leaning over to kiss Crafty on his cheek. "It reminds me of our first date. You remember?"

"Yeah I remember," Crafty replied, eyeing Mayhem as he took a kneeling position between the two cars. "That sucka owed me ten grand and tried hiding out from a brother."

"He was crying like a bitch when we caught him," Bearilla recalled.

"I woulda' been crying too if I got body slammed that hard by a female," Crafty chimed back in.

"That shit looked like it hurt. You damn near broke homeboy's back slamming him across that bench."

Crafty took notice of Mayhem sending him the two finger look signal. Crafty peered through his passenger's side mirror to see a man standing on his front porch smoking a cigarette. Crafty hunched his shoulders to indicate no concern, Mayhem didn't feel Crafty's sentiments.

Crafty answered the incoming call on his two way.

"If cuzz standing there when the brothers come out, I'm laying him down," Mayhem said.

"Stay posted and cover the brothers. We'll handle dude when the time comes," Crafty ordered.

Crafty directed Bearilla to take the man out if he was still present when the brothers were enroute back to the truck.

Crafty was getting ready to radio the Bag brothers when he and Bearilla began hearing lights screams.

"We're on the way out with the coroner," Kid bags spoke across the radio.

"Hold up! We got an innocent bystander," Crafty returned. "Give 'em a minute. He should be done with that cigarette any second."

COP KILLAS II, RENEWED JUSTICE

"I can infared him from here," Mayhem spoke, joining the radio conversation.

"He's going back in the house now," Bearilla told.

"Okay Kid y'all can bring the coroner out," Crafty directed.

Mayhem shifted his position to the side of the house scanning the block for potential problems as the Bag brothers dragged the kicking and screaming coroner out the front door. The coroner gave a fierce struggle as he yelled for help. Mayhem quickly joined the pair using the butt of his rifle to silence the screaming coroner by smashing the back of the coroner's head.

The trio rushed the coroner in the truck as a couple of neighbor's lights came on. Crafty screeched the tires of the truck and sped off the block.

~

DA and the squad sat in the truck discussing the best way to penetrate the ex-mayor's mansion. Once they had their plan together the group hussled from the truck scaling the smaller wall to the side of the property. The crew made entrance through the back patio doors that were unlocked. They began their search for the mayor on the lower level of the mansion. The lower level of the mansion was nearly haunted house dark except for the few dimly lit areas that gave little illumination throughout.

The crew took caution as they moved about. The ex-mayor's house was nice even in the dark. Expensive portraits lined the walls, elegant vases and sculptures sat in most corners, and Cherrywood and Oak furniture decorated the floors.

Not finding the ex-mayor, the crew re-gathered at the bottom of the massive columned staircase. They headed upstairs to continue their search.

The crew checked room by room until they found the master bedroom. The ex-mayor sat up in bed watching the nightly news as the crew entered the threshold. The ex-mayor's eyes scrutinized every man and woman's face as they emerged into the light of his room; he remained cool as ice as the heavily armed group took stance in front of him.

"Let me take a guess at what brings you here," the ex-mayor remarked, glancing back up to his ceiling mounted television while he continued to munch on a can of Pistachios. "It could only be one of three things," he continued, reaching for a glass of water on an adjoining night stand, taking a swig and returning the glass to the stand. "The

Commission, The Police League or both. In either case, I ain't telling you cocksuckers shit. You enter my home unannounced like you're Delta Squad 6 or some fucking body and you're nothing more than mere armed niggers, who just so happen to be breaking THE FUCKING LAW!!

"Fuck the law," Dana blurted, moving towards the side of the ex-mayor's bed.

"And fuck you too," Pockets added, coolly moving to a position on the far side of the bed.

"You idiots put a finger on me and I promise I'll watch cheerfully when my boys feed you to the rats and dogs," The ex-mayor threatened.

"For some strange reason you seem to think you've been promised time," DA spoke, stepping closer to the foot of the bed. "You haven't. You either tell us what we wanna know or you'll be the one fed to the rats…fuckin' cracka."

The room became eerily silent in that moment. Mike, Belinda and Sharon's training kicked in, and they began searching the room for clues.

"Why don't you two give our ex-mayor here a light interrogation," DA ordered, giving Pockets and Dana the ok to get rough. "Mike, take Belinda and Sharon, find his office and tear that fucka apart. I'm gon sit right here and watch our esteemed ex-mayor get his hard skin softened."

"You son's of bitches will regret this," the ex-mayor swore, right before the sound of Dana's right hand slap announced the arrival of the reddest hand print seen on a human cheek before.

The ex-mayor went into hysteria, screaming, kicking and fussing. DA walked away from the bed and out to the balcony as Pockets and Dana began their implementation of ass kicking.

DA radioed the other group for their position, taking a seat on the sturdy and expensive balcony bench.

DA took note of the huge balcony with massive flower plants and as his smile suggested, *rich people shit.*

Kid Bags answered the radio transmission, noting the capture, removal and transport of the coroner. They were less than five minutes away from DA's location and heading back to compound. DA acknowledged the information and clipped the walkie talkie back to his vest. Sharon came through on the small two way radio.

"DA we're in his office two doors down. He has laptop and need we need his code," Sharon instructed.

"Hold tight. I'll have it for you in second," DA responded.

DA was about to relay the message when he heard several bushes crackling. Instinct dropped him to one knee. He spied the area; someone was coming.

"We got company approaching through the back yard," DA whispered, into his two way. "Ladies cover the stair case. Anyone gets in, fire their ass up. Men cover the backyard. Let's send these devils back to hell."

The sound of DA's AR-15 going off initiated the war. Pockets knocked out the ex-mayor with a blow to his chin from the rifle stock and rushed into the next room joining the fight from the balcony as Mike's AR-15 began to scream out from the ex-mayor's office.

"It must be a dozen of them muthafuckas," Mike yelled, killing one of the three advancing masked assassins.

"Minus two," DA returned, witnessing the brutality of his own headshot.

"Make that minus three," Pockets declared, chopping the third man down.

D. MANN

The masked assassins began laying down suppression fire while their team attempted to recover their wounded men. Debris from stucco and glass sprayed the air creating a thick fog like film making sight impossible. Hundreds of shells decimated the décor of the extravagant home and balcony area. Round after round, assassins with fresh clips kept DA, Pockets and Mike subdued; they bunkered down and returned short burst when possible.

"We have to get down stairs to help the men," Sharon screamed, over the sounds of rapid gunfire. "They're out gunned."

Sharon pointed her automatic rifle and hurried down the staircase with Belinda and Dana in close tow. Sharon knelt at the bottom of the staircase using the thick column as cover. She could see assassins through the large patio windows in two group formations; they were successfully dragging their dead from the scene.

Sharon motioned by hand for Belinda to advance and Dana to take the position she currently held. Sharon moved next to the patio window on the opposite side of Belinda.

"We got yo' back bruh," Dana spoke, through the two way.

COP KILLAS II, RENEWED JUSTICE

Dana sprayed the patio door windows shattering them and the three women began their assault. The assassins were taken by surprise and made a partial retreat.

"Hold that position! We're coming down," DA returned. "Brothers fall back!"

DA scurried back inside the room, hoisted the unconscious ex-mayor over his shoulder and made his way out the room. He linked up with Pockets and Mike at the staircase and all three men hurried down the stairs.

"We moving out," Mike yelled, tapping Dana's shoulder and taking her position. "Fall back Dana."

Pockets situated himself next to Mike open firing on anything moving outside.

"Get to the truck now!" Mike shouted, firing his rifle. "We right behind y'all!"

Sharon opened the front door while Belinda and Dana readied themselves to kill any assassins in sight.

"It's clear," Belinda called out, placing herself outside the door.

Dana mimicked Belinda's stance as she posted herself on the opposite side of the door. Sharon made her way to the front gate, pushing the button mounted to the stone pillars that opened it. Dana and Belinda quickly followed.

"We outta here," DA howled. "Let's go y'all."

"Take off first," Mike ordered, Pockets. "I'll be right on your back."

Pockets made his way towards the door. Something moved in the dark hallway that led to another part of the house.

"Assassins in the house," Pockets alerted, spraying the hallway with bullets. "Mike let's go! I got your cover right here."

Mike slid across the hallway path as Pockets kept the assassins at bay. The two men backed their way out the house and continued walking backwards towards the gate. Dana and Belinda noticed the backwards peddle of Mike and Pockets, and took position by the columned gate.

"Let's go gentlemen. We got your cover," Belinda yelled, firing her weapon at the front door forcing the following assassins to take cover inside the mansion.

Sharon pulled the truck pass the gate and ordered the crew to come on. Mike and Pockets hustled to the truck. Belinda grabbed Dana's shoulder as she cross behind her and the two women jumped in the truck and Sharon burned rubber fleeing the scene. The assassins quickly ran out the front gate firing multiple shots at the fleeing truck in attempt to stop it, but to no avail.

Private security finally arrived at the scene to investigate the barrage of gunshots heard throughout the neighborhood. They encountered two men standing in the road; one speaking into a walkie talkie. The two men identified themselves as officers. As soon as the private security let their guards down they were ambushed and killed.

Sharon sped the Suburban through the streets on her way back to the freeway. Everyone was expecting to be chased but not a single vehicle followed them as they rolled along for the next thirty minutes.

Pandemonium broke out when the sound of bullets ricocheting off the truck began. The crew feverishly looked around for their attackers but no one was visible on the road. It wasn't until a bright light from above shined that they noticed the private helicopter with two gun men hovering above them.

"Drop the back window some," Pockets commanded. "I'm on 'em, I'm on 'em!"

D. MANN

Dana, Belinda and Mike cracked their windows far enough the stick their rifle barrels out the window and also return fire.

Sharon accelerated and swerved the road trying to flee the attack helicopter who shadowed their every move as they sped along. The helicopter menaced the truck by flying low and sometimes flying directly in their path.

DA grabbed his walkie talkie and began giving commands.

"Before we get to the compound stop or slow down!" DA instructed. We got something for those bitches."

Sharon sped along trying to out run the pursuing helicopter only to feel her vehicle smashed from the side.

"Aaahhh! We're the fuck they come from?" Belinda screamed, firing her weapon at the truck located on the side of them.

A black truck pulled to their side and attempted to run Sharon's SUV off the road. The two trucks continued to collide as they raced along the road. Occupants from both trucks fired guns at one another. DA's crew shot at the truck and swooping airship. Belinda's aim found its mark as she pierced the others truck's back tire.

COP KILLAS II, RENEWED JUSTICE

The assassin's truck lost control and went careening off into a major boulder that sat off to the side of the desert road. The high speed of the truck caused it to explode in flames upon contact. The crew's attention focused back on the helicopter as Sharon continued to speed down the road.

The helicopter's light was struck by returning fire and knocked out making it difficult to see the airship. The firing guns were the only illumination to indicate the helicopter's position.

"DA the compound is less than two miles away!" Sharon advised.

The helicopter rose to a higher elevation to avoid the guns from the speeding suburban. The airship was out of range from ground attack but still firing at the racing truck.

"DA, we got y'all in sight," Ronald voiced, through the walkie talkie. "Just keep straight."

~

Brazy sat watching the chase through a pair of binoculars as Ronald adjusted the scope on his sniper's rifle. The chase was less than a mile away.

"You better hurry up before they pass us," Brazy urged.

"Tell 'em to stop now!" Ronald ordered.

"Stop the truck!" Brazy yelled, into the two way. "Brake! Brake!"

Sharon heard the command and smashed the brakes bringing the truck to an abrupt stop. The helicopter sat hovering above the truck as the assassins continued to fire on it.

"I got this," Ronald stated, zeroing in on the pilot and firing one shot.

Both men watched as the helicopter began to spin out of control. Ronald made a direct hit. The pilot was mortally wounded and the airship was spinning uncontrolled towards the ground.

Sharon began to move down on the road and all watched as the helicopter started its downward descent.

"Ooh shit they hit it," DA howled, in celebration.

The crew looked on as the helicopter crashed into the desert and exploded killing all on board.

"Ooo wee. Promise me blood you gon' show me use that fucka," Brazy demanded, through his excitement.

"No problem my young brother," Ronald agreed.

Sharon finished driving the rest of the mile and made a right turn into the compound, pulling the truck into the warehouse. Ronald and Brazy rushed downstairs to welcome the crew back.

"Here," DA called out, pushing the ex-mayor away from himself. "Somebody put this piece of shit with the coroner. They have a lot of catching up to do."

"We got the coroner restrained on the third floor," Nap Bags informed. "He up there pleading to Ben like a coward."

"Good! But he won't be the only one up there pleading though," DA responded.

The ex-mayor was taken by Kid and Nap Bags, everyone else was called to huddle up in the break room for briefing one another on.

D. MANN

Chapter 9

Take It to the Grave!

The Penn, as the room was formidably named by the crew was located in the far corner of the building on the third floor. It was used as a utility room once looking at scrap objects that laid around the three wall shelf system. The room itself was humongous, and it now housed the trembling coroner.

Confined to a heavy metal chair, the coroner sat pleading his innocence. The coroner shook and perspired as if he was experiencing extreme hot and cold temperatures. His lips moved fast making his mumble difficult to comprehend.

Leaning against a table, pushed against the front wall sat Ben Brooks; eating an apple and obviously not buying any of the coroner's lame ass explanations.

"I remember asking you some questions that a reporter name Steven White once brought to my attention some years ago. You remember that, don't you?" Ben chastised, calmly and slowly ingesting the remainder of his apple.

COP KILLAS II, RENEWED JUSTICE

Ben began his stroll around the coroner, placing the apple core on the coroner's bobbling head.

"It's amazing how quick he changed his story," Ben taunted, watching the coroner shake the apple core off his head. "The same way you did Carey Henderson, coroner to the stars, kiss ass for the right price!"

"I did my job," the coroner responded, sobbing.

"Bullshit," Ben declared, coolly. "It's funny how one minute you were leaning, oh excuse me, the term you used when speaking out early to Steven White was, 'it's looking like a homicide.' But by the time the press was able to get a camera in your face, you were calling it a suicide. Councilmen Hynes deserved better than that Carey and you know it. You don't want to tell the truth I understand but know this, what goes around comes around.

The coroner hung his head low and continued his light sobbing.

"Sounds like you're about to get some old companionship," Ben stated, listening to the oncoming commotion out in the hallway as he leaned back against the table.

The door swung open and the Bag brothers brought in the frail but resisting ex-mayor. They placed the ex-mayor's seat a foot from the coroners, side by side and confined him to it.

"I'll leave you two to catch up on old times," Ben told, exiting the room with the Bag brothers.

"Y'all be cool," Kid bags warned.

"And try and stay put," Nap Bags joked, closing the door. "Don't go anywhere."

"Well if it isn't Carey Henderson," the ex-mayor started, scrutinizing the coroner's appearance from head to toe. "Seeing that you've pissed your pants already, I guess it's not a far stretch of the imagination to know you've ran your mouth. How much have you told those niggers?"

"Fuck you! I haven't told them shit," the coroner replied. "You're probably the reason these bastards have us here."

"You're spouting off nonsense," the ex-mayor replied. "Just make sure you keep your mouth shut and maybe, just maybe you'll make it out of this alive."

"None of us are making it out of here alive," The coroner exclaimed. "I've already overheard our fate and survival isn't part of it."

"Hmm. You've always been a coward and it's really showing now Carey," the ex-mayor sounded off. "You either take it to the grave with you or you're going in a box sooner than you think."

The coroner hung his head and closed his eyes. He wondered if there was a chance he could come out of this alive. Only time would tell.

Chapter 10

A Lack of Cooperation

"Y'all two muthafuckas gon' tell me exactly what I need to know or y'all gon' be sippin' on testicle soup," DA threatened, slapping blood from the coroner's mouth like a prostitute while eyeing the ex-mayor. "Y'all understand me!"

DA grabbed the ex-mayor around his neck indenting his thumbs and fingers, and began cutting off of the man's air supply. The ex-mayor began gasping and heaving like a wounded man on a battle field.

"Am I making myself fuckin' clear to you!" DA growled, choking the visible life from the ex-mayor.

Crafty, Mike and Ronald quickly set out to restrain DA before he actually killed the ex-mayor without the crew questioning him.

"Let him do his thang!" Pockets roared, rushing to and pulling on Mike's shoulder. "Let him do his thang!"

Dana had straddled Crafty's back in protest of restraining her brother.

"Get y'all hands of my brother!" Dana yelled, tugging on Crafty's massive arms. "He know what he doing!"

"Dana stop!" Crafty barked, yanking at DA's torso. "Dude's eyes rolling back in his head!"

"Fuck 'em! They both guilty!" Dana retorted, still tugging at Crafty's arms.

"DA! LET 'EM GO!" the trio of Crafty, Mike and Ronald screamed, struggling to pry DA's hands from the ex-mayor's throat.

"DA chokin' da shit outta cuzz," Mayhem snickered, laughing out loud.

"Bearilla, Fingers, Brazy and Bloodstone agreed in unison with hysterical laughter that had them falling against one another.

"He about to kill Blood," Brazy giggled, bending over and grabbing his stomach.

"Dat muthafucka's face red as a muthafucka' blood," Bloodstone chuckled, bumping shoulders with Fingers.

"Look at da' coroner cuzz!" Fingers cackled, slapping Brazy's back. "He scared shitless."

"Damnnnn! DA really chokin' da shit outta dat cracka," Bearilla chuckled, but starting to witness the severity of DA's anger.

Elliot, Sharon and Belinda stood, faces solemn as they watched the youthful group visually enjoy a near death sighting as if it was Stand Up Comedy. The young group rolled around in painful laughter.

"DA, my young brother," the elder Ben Brooks uttered, reaching out and touching DA's shoulder calmly. "If I may? It's been quite some time since I've seen these two. If they don't start talking to me, I'll step aside and let you resume your personal style of interrogation. Please young brother, let me talk to them first?"

DA's hands began to ease from around the ex-mayor throat as Ben kept words flowing through his ear. DA let the ex-mayor go but offered a stern warning first.

"You two either talk to him or deal with me. You muthafuckas got one hour; not a second more," DA notified, strolling out of the room with most of the group behind him.

"I guess this is where the past comes back to haunt you ex-mayor Riley," Ben uttered, staring into the eyes of both men. "It's no better time for truth than right now."

"Go to hell Ben," Riley spoke, spitting at the shoes of Ben while his eyes continued to water from the choking. "You and your wanna be paramilitary clowns are as good as dead men for this."

Ben just smiled and walked circles around the two ignoring the threats made by the ex-mayor.

"You know it's a reason I never voted for you," Ben informed. "Stupidity always seemed to be your strong suit to me and I see nothing has changed over the years."

"Save the speech Ben. I'm not telling you a thing," Riley shot back, slowly regaining his breath.

"Have it your way. Maybe you should save what little breath my brother kindly left you," Ben stated, leaning against the table. "But understand when my young brother gets back in here, not even Jesus will be able to save you."

"Fuck the both of you," ex-mayor Riley declared.

"How about you Carey? You're not talking either?" Ben asked.

"I don't know anything," Carey replied, looking nervous and clearing his mouth of still forming blood.

"Of course you do," Ben returned. "All those obvious murders,"

"They were suicides!" the coroner Carey screamed, spitting into a small pool of blood forming between his feet.

"Yeah! Once you were elected to do the autopsy," Ben enlightened, with his intense tone. "Just like you called Councilmen Hynes and Jackson's murders a suicide! Who ordered you to do so?"

The coroner sat silent with his head hung low. He attempted to avoid any eye contact with Ben. Ben pushed himself off the table, walked over to Carey, grabbed his chin and raised his head. Ben's stare told of bad things to come.

"Who ordered you to cover up their murders?" Ben questioned, sternly.

The coroner gazed in the eyes of Ben. For a brief moment his eyes peeked over at the ex-mayor. Ben caught the glance.

"Was it you Riley? Were you the one giving the coroner his orders?" Ben inquired. "You were definitely banker funded and operated."

Both men sat defiantly quiet as Ben gave them the evil stare down. Ben continued to question the two men for nearly a hour without any progress or admissions from either. The vast sounds of boots were heard approaching at a rapid pace. Ben shook his head at the lying pair.

"From the sounds of it," Ben said, cuffing his ear with an apparent smile on his face. "This lack of cooperation just qualified you two for a well whooped ass," Ben finished, opening the door.

Chapter 11

Discovery

"We gotta another hit!" Ronald screamed, with Brazy slapping his shoulder as several members of the team gathered around. "Thanks to the Bag brothers introduction of Henry Robertson we've been able to find some key information."

"And a few more guilty faces," Brazy added.

"It seems that Henry Robertson and Casey Kovac partnered in very lucrative business transactions here in Los Angeles during the late 70's and early 80's. They used many principle banks for revenue adjustment and the Commission for control and guaranteed licensing," Ronald spoke, spinning in his chair from the laptop screen to eye the group with his look of sincerity. "They owned LA's business sector."

Ronald spun back around facing the excited Brazy and requested he pull up cross references.

"Blood I learned how to cross reference. You know I'm classified G-14 now right? Check this shit out," Brazy announced, flashing laptop screens.

COP KILLAS II, RENEWED JUSTICE

"These are all known business associates and all unknown business associates for both Henry Robertson and Casey Kovac," Ronald explained, as Brazy readied himself to switch screens again. "A few things to make note of. Most are dead, most had numerous shell companies and almost all took out investment loans with these banking institutions here."

Brazy's finger tapped a key and a flash introduced new details.

"Damn blood! That's a lot of banks," Bloodstone acknowledged, squinting as his head leaned forward.

"I count about two dozen myself," Sharon stated.

"Mmm hmmm," Brazy agreed, glancing at Sharon.

"Yeah but after cross referencing loan amounts to these dudes shell companies you find out these four banks continually approved the biggest loans with or without city approval," Ronald added, as Brazy changed screens again. "These are the four men that ran those banks; they were all Financial Analysts. All decease, all four by suicide."

"Suicide my ass cuzz," Fingers grunted, tapping Belinda's arm. "Dem muthafuckas got smoked! You feel me?"

"Yeah. Unfortunately I do," Belinda answered, retreating to her own mind momentarily. "Are any of these banks still in operation now because somebody is still funding these assholes?"

"Don't know but we'll find out soon," Ronald replied. "What I can tell you is this, one of Casey Kovac's last transactions before his demise a few years back was a joint endeavor with our current head of Police League and ex-police chief Darryl Fince himself.

"The rest of the group needs to hear this right now," Crafty urged.

"My uncles, DA, Mike and Elliot are still on radio silence," Bearilla responded, hugging Crafty's shoulders. Dana and Pockets are out on the premises somewhere doing the nasty I bet."

"At a time like this you can think about sex?" Crafty questioned, in disbelief.

"At a time like this you could be getting," Bearilla teased, going into an ear whisper that put a smile across Crafty's face.

Crafty looked at his watch. DA and the others wouldn't be heard from for another twenty minutes, they were maintaining strict radio silence for their current mission.

It had been awhile since Crafty had the pleasure of enjoying his woman's company and Bearilla was pushing her sexual agenda to full extent down on Crafty.

"I'll be back in twenty minutes," Crafty advised, grabbing Bearilla by the hand and dragging her in a hurry out of the room.

Crafty figured the third floor, south corner of complex 3 would present a nice quiet spot for him and Bearilla to spend some quality time until the sounds of Dana and Pockets emanated from a room up ahead.

"Sounds like your little homeboy on his knees," Bearilla commented, with a wide smile across her face. "And I don't think he's proposing."

"Probably not," Crafty responded, escorting Bearilla to the opposite side of the building. "But it sure sounds like she's saying yes; over, over and over again. You'll be joining her as soon as we get in a room."

Chapter 12

Understood!

The Bag brothers dragged the unconscious man down the hall followed by DA, Elliot and Mike. Ben stood in the doorway with a rising smile as he stepped aside to allow entrance. The ex-mayor and coroner's eyes grew ten centimeters when the brothers pulled the man through the door.

DA grabbed a chair from the back of the room, placing it next to the ex-mayor and the Bag brothers started to confine the man wit cuffs and shackles to it.

DA gave a quick inspection of his watch and steadied the brothers as they put the finishing touches on confining the man.

"Times up for you fuckas!" DA alerted, posturing in front of the flinching ex-mayor who sat in the middle chair while the shaking coroner remembered the previous blood drawing strike DA gave to his mouth. "I hope y'all had something tell Ben."

"Neither one felt like telling me anything," Ben replied, watching Elliot make his way over to the unconscious man.

COP KILLAS II, RENEWED JUSTICE

"John Whitecloud!" Elliot yelled, slapping the unconscious man awake. The man's body jolted back to life. "Wake yo' punk ass up! I always wanted to say that."

Ben began giving John Whitecloud a brief update on his current position and problem. The group sat around looking on as Ben refreshed John on his personal history. John took note of his environment and the two men seated next to him. John Whitecloud became extremely nervous.

"Let me make a long story short for you," Ben said, leaning back against the table. "These men want to know who pulled your chain back then."

John Whitecloud scanned the faces of the men who stood before him; they looked as if they wanted him dead.

"Now I know your first mind is tell us fuck us and you're not telling us shit," Ben told. "But I would seriously advise against that. You're in the presence of some real live niggas with attitudes. Each one of them waiting to peel a piece of skin from your fake Indian white racist ass. My advice would be to talk and talk fast. Time is up as my young brother told those two a minute ago."

"That was all so long ago. What's your personal interest?" John asked, looking in the eyes of DA.

"From the looks of it, that was before your time son."

"The Arrington's," DA announced, flashing back to his parents while moving to face John Whitecloud, and smacking him in similar fashion to the ex-mayor. "And I'm asking the fucking questions around here; remember that!"

DA eyed the coroner and ex-mayor and walked back over in front of the ex-mayor.

"Nobody wants to make a deal huh?" DA asked, scanning between the three men.

All three men sat quietly with their faces down. DA without hesitation pulled his pistol from his side holster and fired one shot into the ex-mayor's skull, killing him instantly. John Whitecloud and the coroner went into a frantic hysteria, screaming and crying.

"Shut the fuck up!" DA ordered, slapping John Whitecloud with his pistol and missing a swipe at the coroner's head. DA stood erect after regaining his balance from the stumble leaning across the ex-mayor's body. "Y'all either tell me something or die right now!"

Mike and Elliott rushed DA to halt his killing spree while the Nap Brothers studied the growing tussle.

"DA we need these assholes!" Mike screamed, struggling with DA.

DA broke free from the grasping Mike and Elliot pointing his pistol in the face of Mike.

"Don't get confused!" DA shouted. "This joint operation or whatever the fuck you wanna call it is under my control! This will be the last time I ask you if we clear on that!"

"I'm just saying don't kill everybody before we get a chance to find out something," Mike returned, moving his head from in front of DA's pistol. "Our lives are in jeopardy just as well as yours. Hell, let the little psycho at least torture the fucks first."

DA slowly returned his pistol to his side holster taking his stare from Mike and placing it on the two confined men.

"Y'all gon' stay true to not divulging secrets?" Ben inquired.

Both men continued to staunchly plead their innocence sobbing they were only doing their jobs. DA pulled his two way radio and put out a call of urgency to Pockets with a message to bring his trade tools immediately.

~

Dana sat with her head in Pocket's chest listening to him detail his love for her.

"I got your back," Pockets admitted, kissing her forehead. "I have to die before something can happen to you. I'll kill anything that becomes a threat to you. I love you girl."

"I know you do baby," Dana acknowledged. "I love you too and when I see that bitch Taquisha again, I'm gon' put her triflin' ass in a box for slippin' you the eye. I ain't forgot about that nasty hoe. She gon' regret trying to steal my man."

"Girl stop being crazy," Pockets spoke laughing. "We involved wit some serious shit here. I want you to know I mean every word I say."

"You know I'm gon' be your wife one day," Dana demanded.

"Yeah I know," Pockets agreed. "And you know I'm gon' be yo' husband."

"To death do we part," Dana stated, with a smile on her face.

"To death," Pockets followed.

"Yo' hard ass like all this mushy shit don't you?" Dana teased, poking Pockets in his side.

The two way radio that laid on the table began to send static noise across the room.

"Pockets. I need you in The Penn now! Bring your trade tools," DA's voice came across the two way radio.

"On my way," Pockets spoke, back into the two way radio. "I guess they back."

"Let's go see what's up," Dana urged, leading the way out of the room.

~

Pockets and Dana strolled into the room to the smiles of the group.

"Pockets these muthafuckas need an incentive to talk," DA growled, walking over to the couple and placing his arm around Dana. "Baby girl come with me. I wanna talk to you about something."

DA, Dana, Ben, Mike and Elliot left the room leaving Pockets to his craft with the Bag brothers as observers.

Pockets cleared the table with one wiping fashion and began to roll out his bag of toys. He studied the instruments while peeking at the two remaining survivors who were now sweating from the sight of Pockets' weapons.

D. MANN

The Bag brothers laid their backs against the wall, crossing their arms in unison. They studied the young Pockets trademenship with scrutiny.

Pockets fingered over the tools he rolled out his bag wrap and glanced at the two squirming men again.

"I swear to you young man; I'm innocent!," the coroner swore sobbing. "I only did my job. Why won't anyone listen to me!"

Kid Bag leaned over and whispered in the ear of his brother Nap. Pockets spotted the quick exchange of whispers between the brothers, knelt down, fumbled through his roll along case and spied the desperate two again.

"Young man you don't want to do this!" John Whitecloud cried out, locking eyes with Pockets. "You don't want to die from lethal injection and that's exactly what they'll give you for killing retired officials. Besides, I truly am innocent. I've never been convicted of any crime."

Nap Bags kept a stern face as he barely allowed a sign of smirking to be noticed on his lips when Pockets met his glance.

Pockets retrieved a roll of duct tape from his roll along, walked over and taped both men's ligaments at the elbows, shoulders and knees to the chairs they were cuffed and shackled to.

The Bag brothers quickly went into a huddle watching Pockets secure the still screaming and pleading men. They both looked confused to Pockets' methods.

After a final tightness inspection Pockets walked back over to his roll along case and fumbled through it again.

Pockets withdrew a hand full of nails and a hammer from his roll along, turning to face the two men with his homemade look of ensuing terror. His head swayed back and forth between the two begging men.

The brothers glared at Pockets choice of weapons and went into a smiling conference. They approved. Pockets could hear Nap Bags uttered the phrase 'old school.'

Pockets stepped forward towards John Whitecloud. He placed the nail on the top of his trembling knee cap and pounded the hammer down on top of the nail with force.

After the initial shriek of agonizing pain and thirty second cry that followed, John Whitecloud began hyperventilating and passed out. Pockets stare at Carey menaced the coroner's heart; he began yelling his innocence again.

The Bag brothers were impressed with Pockets implementation and it showed as the brothers gave constant head nods during their conference.

"I thought it was a threat," Kid Bags admitted, showing signs of excitement.

"I thought it was a threat too," Nap Bags agreed, showing his own signs of euphoria. "But he ain't say one got damn word!"

"Yeah!" Kid Bags acknowledged, giving his brother's fist a pound from his own. "He got right to that shit."

Nap Bags gave the hmmm face as Pockets prepared himself to drive a nail through the imploring coroner's shoulder.

"Please! I'll tell the other man whatever he wants to know," the coroner pleaded. "Please! I'll tell you sir. Please! Let me help. I want to help you!"

"You wanna help us?" Pockets questioned, freezing his impending swing of the hammer. "For real for real?"

"Yes," Carey whined. "I want justice from these pricks too. I suffered unjust scrutiny and nearly lost my career behind these assholes and their crooked dealings."

"Somebody call DA and let 'em know the coroners ready to talk," Pockets ordered, turning and smashing another nail through the coroner's shoulder with one quick bang of his hammer.

"Ahhh!" Carey screamed, as tears and sweat streamed down his face.

"Oooh," Kid Bags spoke, in awe covering his mouth. "He did it again."

"I didn't see it coming," Nap Bags uttered, pulling his two way radio.

Nap Bags made the call to DA. DA was pleased to hear whimpering and groaning in the background.

"I thought he was going to let him get away with it after he agreed to talk," Kid Bags guessed.

"Young bruh a natural!" Nap Bags replied.

Pockets grabbed the coroner around his throat giving him a warning.

"Waste my time and I swear I'll drive the next nail through the top of your fucking head. You understand me!" Pockets yelled, backing away from the coroner. "You understand me?"

"Yes," Carey replied, sobbing. "I understand."

"Brothers, one of y'all mind waking that bitch up," Pockets asked, applying a forceful pull and yanking the nail in one fluid motion out of Carey's shoulder.

Carey the coroner yelled as the sweat and tears continued to drench his face. He was sobbing worse than when the nail entered his shoulder.

"Yeah I got you young bruh," Kid Bags responded, stepping over and pimp slapping the unconscious John Whitecloud a couple times until he regained consciousness. John Whitecloud began to scream as soon as he awakened.

COP KILLAS II, Renewed Justice

Chapter 13

Pressing Business

DA and Dana listened intensively as Belinda, Ronald and Brazy shared new information.

"It seems our Darryl Fince is the boss man of this mischief," Ronald informed. "But his second in charge is the one who took the rap when the heat came down."

"Jim Hernandez spent three years in prison and was fired by the department. Since then he has kept a low profile but we found him living in Agoura Hills," Belinda interrupted. "It seems like he still in good grace with the chief."

"Fall guy with benefits huh," DA guessed, retreating back into his mind.

"Jim Hernandez got his self crossed up when he got caught taking a bribe from a then mid-level banker named Adam Fince," Brazy added.

"Adam Fince! He related to the chief?" Dana inquired.

"Uh huh," Brazy answered.

"So the ex-Chief of Police has a brother in the banking industry," Mike uttered.

"You said mid-level banker," DA repeated. What the banker's name who was in authority?" DA questioned.

Ronald tapped the keys and the screen blinked.

"Simon Davenport," Ronald told. "He was bank president at First Republic back then."

"First Republic!" Dana responded. "Downtown LA?"

"Yup," Ronald replied.

DA and Dana both peered at one another thinking the same thing.

"Where is this Simon now?" DA asked.

Ronald began tapping on the keys again.

"Hollywood Hills Cemetery," Ronald replied. "Seems he caught a real bad case of lead poisoning; One shot to the head. Of course it was declared a suicide. But look at this," Ronald continued, reading his laptop screen. "It seems that Simon was the star witness for the prosecution before his demise. He was ready to scapegoat his underling Adam Fince the same way Darryl Fince scapegoated his underling Jim Hernandez."

"Most likely Darryl Fince had Simon Davenport silenced to protect his brother Adam," Belinda figured, running thoughts through her mind. "You remember Sharon told us that a lot of the info she found was provided by an anonymous source."

"What your point?" Ronald asked.

"Well it seems this unknown person was passing along information that was responsible for getting several key people killed," Belinda speculated.

"The bankers were the only one who avoided prosecution with the exception of Simon Davenport," DA informed, thinking again to himself. "We should start a new search on the banks connected to the Fince brothers. I think it's possible that's where we'll find the missing link at."

"I think you might be right DA," Ronald agreed. "We'll get on it right now."

DA received a radio transmission requesting his presence in the Penn and him and Dana walked out of the room. DA and Dana strolled the final corridor exchanging their insights.

"Baby girl, I think it's time we go visit moms and see what she remembers," DA suggested. "It was her boss that got murdered."

"Yeah a road trip is definitely in order," Dana agreed. "Moms might remember some shit she didn't think was important at the time."

"We'll take care of that once we finish this," DA recommended, opening the door and allowing Dana to enter the room first.

"Oh boy can't wait to tell you everything he knows," Pockets told, pointing at the coroner as DA closed the door. "And Johnny here has a few pieces of information he wants to share too."

"The young brother was super convincing," Nap Bags interjected.

"Who's talking first?" DA asked, switching views between the two confined men.

The coroner starting pouring out his story first.

"Darryl Fince threatened to have my family murdered if I didn't constantly validate his point of view," The coroner said, beginning to cry again. "I was scared these bastards would kill my family; it wasn't the first time they've killed. I've never harmed anyone."

"What were your orders?" DA asked.

"Falsify any documents I was instructed to," the coroner answered, solemnly. "I was usually approached by Jim Hernandez or a slew of lesser ups demanding I follow strict orders."

"You've been working there for twenty years Carey!" DA growled, stepping forward towards the coroner. "You must've falsified thousands of documents!"

Saliva from DA's mouth spattered across Carey's face as DA yelled, nearly nose to nose with the coroner. The coroner was so terrified he never felt DA's spittle drip from his top lip.

"Did you falsify the Arrington's death certificate too?" DA questioned, at the top of his lungs.

The question had taken the coroner back in time. DA studied his face and demeanor. The coroner looked visibly distraught as he flashed back.

"Call it a foolish belief if you want but I really believed the young couple had a chance to destroy that system," the coroner spoke, with his head hanging.

"Answer the got damn question Carey fo' I lose my fuckin' control!" DA demanded.

"Yes," the coroner answered, exhaling deeply.

Dana sprang forward.

"Those were our parents' dead man!" Dana barked, into the coroner's face.

"I know. You favor your mother," the coroner replied, soft spoken and staring in her eyes possibly for sympathy. "Just as your brother here favors your father."

The coroner began to smile and let out a slight sound of laughter.

"I was supposed to be one of their star witnesses," the coroner moaned, tears streaming down his face. "When they initially came to me I told them I wouldn't risk my family and they understood that. They were really decent people. But once they managed to shake up the power structure, I wanted to testify. I wanted to see the untouchables finally get touched. They had them shook up and running scared."

Silence fell on the room as the coroner reminisced briefly.

"I saw them as brave and honorable," the coroner started. "I also saw them as my only way out and I was tired of living under constant threat. Your father once told me that he understood my situation because he had children of his own. For that reason he never tried to pressure me. He agreed once their case was strong enough, I would come forward. They were close to tearing down the Fince brothers reign."

"What about you John?" DA inquired, turning to face the listening John Whitecloud. "Why don't you tell me who lined your pockets throughout the years?"

"Most of it was hand to hand cash transfers," John Whitecloud began, looking sorrowful. "But the money was coming from the bankers and their investors; private investors etc. Everyone knew if you wanted to do something in Los Angeles, you had to sit down with the Fince brothers. They ran the city with money and force."

The group continued to listen without any expressions of sympathy.

"Once your parents got a hold of Simon Davenport the green light was given to take them and Davenport out," John stated. "Your parents were gifted some damaging information on Davenport's sexual discretions to force their will. Simon Davenport was a prestigious and upstanding man of the community and the tarnishing of his character would bring embarrassment to his fellow elites. His circle couldn't allow their activities to come to light. It was rumored that he had a weakness for young women of other races and his specialty…teenage stud boys. It seemed that

Davenport and his crowd favored the dark meat, and that was the very information used to force his hand."

"You said gifted," Nap Bags interjected, still laying his back against the wall. "By who?"

"No one ever knew for sure," John answered, turning his face to eye the calm Nap Bags. "It had to be someone in his circle and someone who hated him bad. They gave up all the goods on him. Davenport was as good as done from that point on."

"What were your specific orders John?" DA asked. "And who gave 'em to you."

"I received cash to vote certain ways on projects that didn't meet the city's strict criteria. Mostly for new developments," John explained. "It was either take the cash or receive a bullet."

"It that your excuse John Whitecloud?" Kid Bags inquired.

"The bankers and the investors were going to have their way; one way or another. And I didn't see the need to be the next councilman to end up in a custom built box," John responded. "It was solely my reason."

COP KILLAS II, RENEWED JUSTICE

"Once again who gave you your orders?" Pockets asked, squeezing the back of John's neck with an extra tight grip.

"Depends," John replied, squinting his eyes from the neck tightening pressure of Pockets' squeeze.

"On what?" DA urged, focusing in on John's now narrow eyes.

"The deal itself," John told, with pleading eyes. "Sometimes it would be Chief Fince's yes man Dale Harris or one of his crew. Sometimes it would come from bankers or investor's envelope henchmen. They'd show up with instructions and an envelope for payment and I would take it and cast my vote as instructed.

DA eyed the two men silently for all of ten seconds before he backed away still glaring at the two. DA turned, touched Dana's shoulder and headed towards the door.

"What you wanna do with these two DA," Pockets asked, with his hand planted firmly on John Whiteclouds' shoulder.

DA glanced back at the shivering men fathoming his decision.

"Leave 'em be for now," DA ordered. "We'll deal with them later. Right now we all need to regroup. It's time to put a major plan together. We about to bring all this shit to an end."

"Lucky for you two we got pressing business or I'd have y'all asses howling to the moon; howling to da' moon," Pockets commented, following the group out the door with the most sincere look on his face.

Chapter 14

A Bad Connection

"Try mom again DA," Dana requested, studying the battery life of her own phone. "Her phone keep going straight to voicemail and my phone damn near dead."

DA retrieved his phone and tried calling Ms. Williams at her residence and then at the bank. Ms. Williams was non responsive to either line.

Crafty pulled the Suburban truck in the massive circular driveway of Ms. Williams' home and the group exited the truck.

"This a nice ass home!" Bearilla stated, allowing her eyes to take in the one story edifice. "It don't surprise me y'all momma live here. This is why yo' ass so rich and stuck up, huh DA?"

"Yeah. Something like that B," DA answered, with a face that told of Bearilla's question as irrelevant conversation.

Dana rang the doorbell and the group waited along the porch area. No one answered and after a long pause Dana rang the doorbell again. After another two minutes Ms. Williams open the door adorning a fluffy robe and a towel that wrapped her hair like an East Indian.

"Hey my babies," Ms. Williams spoke, excitedly hugging and studying DA and Dana's matching outfits. "Hey Crafty! And who is this young lady? Y'all look nice but militant wearing all this black."

Crafty returned Ms. Williams' hug and introduced Bearilla as his woman name B.

"Thanks," Crafty replied, tugging on the shoulders of his outfit as he stepped through the doorway. "Tight huh?"

"Hi B," Ms. Williams called, laughing and hugging the huge woman. "You can call me momma like everybody else. I see you don't miss too many meals do you?"

"I sure don't," Bearilla responded, stepping through the door threshold with the rest of the group. "And whatchu' got to eat up in the big o' crib momma?"

Ms. Williams closed the door and instructed everyone to follow her into the kitchen. Bearilla excitedly commented on the extensive fine art work that decorated the walls of the hallways that seemed like an intricate maze.

"Dang momma you can get lost in here," Bearilla stated, turning another corner.

"Girl let me tell you," Ms. Williams returned, laughing and continuing to lead the way. "I've gotten lost many of times trying to find my own kitchen."

"Here we go," Ms. Williams uttered, indicating their arrival to the sought room. "Help yourself to the refrigerator B."

Bearilla moved about the kitchen with the speed and dexterity of a professional chef. She was holding a knife and ingredients to a big sandwich within seconds as she headed to the edge of the kitchen isle from the refrigerator.

The group stood like mannequins watching Bearilla's preparation before they scattered across the lavish kitchen for seats.

Ms. Williams walked around the kitchen isle and leaned her elbows on the counter continuing to watch Bearilla's chef skills. "So what bring my babies by? I hope this ain't just a business call."

"Unfortunately it is momma," DA replied, leaning his elbows on the counter directly across from Ms. Williams. "I need you to ask you about a former boss of yours; Simon Davenport."

"Simon Davenport!" Ms. Williams shrieked, snapping her neck backwards as she recalled her past, glancing back over to Bearilla. "There's some Honey Mustard in the cabinets above the utensil drawer B. What about that nasty bastard?"

"Thanks momma," Bearilla stated, rubbing her hands together as she made a quick stroll to the cabinets.

"We need to know of anyone who was a regular in his office or someone he stayed in touch with," DA inquired. "Anything that may have seemed out of place."

"What! Besides the young boys that he kept coming through his revolving door," Ms. Williams informed. "Thanks to that bastard the whole bank went through a restructuring period."

"Restructuring period?" Dana asked, joining the conversation.

"Once sleazy Simon killed himself behind the scandal he caused, the bank's reputation was almost destroyed," Ms. Williams shared. "We went through bank president after bank president. It seemed no one could restore the bank's luster. Of course, I being one of five women working there, only two of us black. I was passed over for another decade before I got my first promotion.

COP KILLAS II, RENEWED JUSTICE

They've always kept a white girl in control. They don't trust nobody outside their own."

"What do you know about the Fince brothers' connection to your bank back then?" DA asked.

"They were always around or having some business meeting with Simon but all that faded away after Simon's death," Ms. Williams replied.

"Who runs the bank now?" DA questioned.

"Stock Holders," Ms. Williams responded. "Which actually turns out to be private investors with very large pockets."

"Can you find out discreetly which investors have been in bed with your bank before and after Simon's death?" DA asked.

"I should be able to with no problem," Ms. Williams acknowledged. "Give me a day or two. I should have something for you."

DA stood up and looked around the kitchen. Everyone was focus on the conversation with the exception of Bearilla who clearing down part of a sandwich with a swallow of milk.

"You sound suspicious of the bank. Did they have something to do with Darryl and Diane's death?" Ms. Williams asked, raising herself up from the counter with an angered look on her face.

"Were Simon and the Fince brothers involved DA?"

"It looks that way but we don't know for sure," DA answered. "We damn sure plan on finding out."

"C'mon y'all we can finish talking in the living room," Ms. Williams ordered, taking lead again and heading towards another pathway connected to the kitchen. "B you can bring the sandwich if you want. We'll be in the living room."

"No need," Bearilla explained, producing a wind causing burp that roared through the spacious kitchen. "I'm done now."

"Just leave the plate and glass in the sink and c'mon," Ms. Williams chuckled. "We don't want to have to send out a search party for you girl."

"You need to find you some food etiquette B," Crafty argued, waving his hand continually back and forth in front of his face as he followed behind her. "That burp smell like turkey shit salad."

"Forget you Crafty!" Bearilla joked, slapping Crafty's shoulder.

The group all laughed as they entered the large and seemingly comfy living room and took seats.

COP KILLAS II, RENEWED JUSTICE

DA, Dana and Crafty brought Ms. Williams up to date on what they had learned over the last couple weeks. Ms. Williams listened intently as she provided some details throughout the discussion. The group had a lot more clarity of the banks position and dealings now that they sat with Ms. Williams. The group sat flabbergasted as Ms. Williams went into detail about the Fince brothers, the bank and private investors.

"These muthafuckas think they can do anything they want," Dana interjected, pounding one fist into the other.

"Don't worry baby girl," DA responded, touching his sister's shoulder for comfort. "Those devils about to experience a bad connection."

"Indeed big bruh," Dana spoke, delighted. "Indeed."

D. MANN

Chapter 15

Epiphany

"We need to find addresses for Casey Kovac and Susan Whitmore ASAP," DA demanded, spinning around in his chair to face the Bag brothers. "I think it's time we talk to Steven White too."

"You want us to pick him up?" Nap Bags asked, leaning closer to DA.

"Naw," DA answered. "Just convince him to talk. They scared him out of a story back then so he'll probably be scared now. Take Pockets and a couple of those youngsters with y'all."

"Cool," Kid Bags replied, to DA calling for Mayhem and Bloodstone with a repetitive hand wave. "We rolling! Find Pockets and tell him to bring his work tools. We downstairs in five minutes."

DA leaned back in his chair and contemplated the next moves of the group. The Bag brothers had given DA a great plan but a dangerous one. Mike and Elliot had come up with a more practical plan but timing and location would be crucial to its success. The rest of the group gave a split decision to either of the plans; DA had to make a choice.

COP KILLAS II, RENEWED JUSTICE

Ronald, Brazy and Belinda sat at the two laptops still on discovery missions. They were searching for the last known locations for two pieces to their puzzle.

DA back tracked over previous information he had learned and pondered over his thoughts. He was certain of the Fince brother's guilt but his gut instinct told him there was someone else that would miss the party he had intended on hosting, if they didn't find the culprit soon.

"What's wrong DA?" Sharon asked, studying DA's face as she entered the room, taking a seat next to him.

"Nothing," DA retorted, sitting up in his chair and shuffling through papers.

DA perused several papers studying some of them intently. It was speculation at its best, but DA's instinct told him there was a Casper playing ghost somewhere.

"I'll tell you what's wrong," Dana blurted out, kicking her feet up on the board room table and gaining the interest of DA and Sharon. "Somebody being messy! I just had an epiphany. Did I say that word right?" "

"Yes you did. What you mean messy?" Sharon inquired, as DA focused in on his younger sister.

"This whole thing!" Dana started, returning DA's stare. "It seems like some typical hood shit. You remember when I told you about dem' two bitches Tara and Nikki getting into it."

"A little," DA whispered, thinking back to the conversation he shared with Dana some time back. "Didn't somebody get smoked behind that shit?"

"Yeah! A few people." Dana exclaimed. "The bitch Nikki's cousin got killed too remember?" Dana didn't give DA a chance to reply. "Nikki and Tara were both sleeping with the same dude name Cisco. Cisco told Tara that he would never leave Nikki and that Nikki was his one first love. That shit sent Tara on one. Tara told some Crips from the eastside that Nikki was the one responsible for setting up their homeboy and getting him killed. Those Crips came back and cleaned house. They paralyzed Nikki from the waist down, killed her cousin, killed Cisco and his best friend. Then after all that it came out that Tara lied trying to get Nikki killed so she could have Cisco to herself."

"So what happen to Tara?" Sharon questioned.

"And how does that story have anything to do with the shit we're working on?" DA interrupted.

"Once the police starting investigating the murders, those Crips went back and killed Tara, her little brother and her auntie who lived with her," Dana stated, figuring DA and Sharon should have figured it out by now.

Dana sat quietly waiting for DA or Sharon to have their, *Ah ha* moment but both sat stone face waiting for the catch.

"Y'all still don't get it?" Dana asked, with a look of disgust on her face.

"Naw baby girl I don't," DA disclosed.

"That muthafucka you call Casper playing ghost is most likely a bitch!" Dana informed, crossing her arms across her chest. "Just think about this. Somebody gets mad for whatever reason and starts dropping dimes; big time snitching. Big names starts taking heat. Sleazy Simon gets caught up with our parents and he's not going down alone; they whack him and a shit storm gets set off. Now you have a bunch of criminal muthafuckas scrambling to kill the skeletons coming out of their closets. I betchu' my last dollar when we find the w-o-m-a-n who started leaking shit, we'll find this shit had nothing to do with criminal cops and dirty bankers. This feels like some of that emotional, *I'm hurt and gon' get revenge type shit.* Watch what I tell you."

"You might be right baby girl," DA uttered, wondering how much of Pockets had rubbed off on his sister.

"I am right," Dana countered.

"That's what's been bothering me," DA confided. "For this to be professionals it seems like everybody involved was acting non-professional and yes I agree baby girl, this shit seems hella messy."

"The question becomes then if it is a woman," Sharon commented. "Is the woman linked to this scandal by business or relationship?"

"I think a better question is," Dana interjected. "Is the woman scorned by business or relationship?"

"That sounds more logical to me," DA joined in. "I have a good feeling if the reporter talks to the Bag brothers we'll be finding out who our Casper the ghost really is."

COP KILLAS II, Renewed Justice

Chapter 16

Who's That Lady?

"DA! We found Susan Whitmore," Belinda told, showing DA a printed out paper. "She died ten months ago of cervical cancer in Seattle, Washington."

"What about Casey Kovac?" DA asked, handing Belinda back the piece of paper.

"We're still trying to find his whereabouts," Belinda answered, turning and heading back to table where the laptops sat. "He flies around the world most of the time now on business. I'll let you know as soon as we find him."

DA thought to himself about Dana's conclusion. It made sense in a weird way. DA decided to take a break from the case to relax his mind but relaxing his mind didn't happen. DA decided to make a quick trip to the Penn. Maybe John Whitecloud knew of something or someone that he didn't figure was important at the time.

DA got up from his seat and walked out of the room followed by Sharon.

"DA! Wait up," Sharon pleaded, trying to catch the fast paced walking DA. "Where you going?"

"I just got a couple more questions for John Whitecloud," DA answered, never breaking his stride.

"I'm going to check out something myself," Sharon notified. "I'll be back shortly. I think I may have overlooked something."

"Take a couple people with you," DA uttered, stopping in his tracks and hugging Sharon. "And be careful, I love you."

"I will," Sharon replied, returning the hug of DA. "I love you too."

The two split and DA continued on his way. DA walked through the door of the Penn, pulled a seat in front of John Whitecloud and the coroner and began his questioning.

"I need you to really think back and tell me about Simon Fince and Casey Kovac," DA ordered, laying his arms stacked across the back of John Whitecloud's chair.

"What do you wanna know?" John Whitecloud spoke.

"I wanna know about the women these two men entertained," DA said. "Anything you can remember from back then."

COP KILLAS II, RENEWED JUSTICE

John Whitecloud went into a spell thinking back to the past. John just shook his head from side to side for a few seconds before the words started spilling from his mouth.

"You know Casey Kovac considered himself quite the ladies' man in his day," John told. "So it wasn't a shock to see him with different woman on any giving day and this guy had a harem full of women. There was this one episode that took place at one of their uppity parties where Susan Whitmore blew up and called Casey out for sleeping with some woman."

"What's so strange about that?" DA inquired. "If he was known for having many women as you say."

"True," John agreed. "But that's what made it so strange. Susan had known about Casey's addictive history with women the entire time so when she blew up, not only was it a shocker, most people took it as a sign that Susan considered this mystery woman as a threat to her power."

"Why?" DA asked.

"The way she complained and cried about the other woman," John emphasized. "She wanted that woman gone and I mean d-e-a-d gone. Susan almost had a stroke at that party."

"Did Susan ever use the woman's name?" DA questioned. "Did she ever reveal the woman's identity?"

"No. Not at all. She refused to," John informed. "But through a racist rant we found out the woman was non-white. She specifically called her a non-white in attempt to embarrass Casey among the white elites he gathered for his party. She never went too far, she made certain not to give a description of the woman's identity. But without using the n-word, I think everyone got the picture."

"Has anyone you know of ever seen this woman?" DA asked.

"No. but it was rumored that this mystery woman had slept with not only Casey but also Simon Davenport," John answered. "For what it's worth, some say she even had Susan under her thumb."

"How so?" DA inquired.

"An alleged lesbian relationship," John offered. "Susan was known to fancy the company of a pretty lady now and then too."

"Wow," DA uttered. "This shit sounds like script from Hollywood."

DA rose from his seat, spent the chair around in his hands and slid the chair back under the table.

COP KILLAS II, RENEWED JUSTICE

DA glared at John Whitecloud for a second until he was interrupted by the coroner calling out young man.

"What is it?" DA answered, sternly walking to the door and pausing.

"There was once an exclusive club; an all woman's club," The coroner explained. "Rich housewives, movie star wives, you know the elite woman's club of Los Angeles."

"Susan Whitmore?" DA speculated, interrupting the coroner.

"Yes, she wasn't exactly open with it, but she wasn't shy about it either," the coroner replied. "It was the same thing with a host of others. Your mystery woman might have frequented the club. It was a v-e-r-y discreet club for women who indulged sexually in other women."

"What was the name of the club?" DA inquired.

"The Eastern Star," the coroner told. "It was named after a Masonic order of elite and lonely white women whose powerful husbands screwed anything with a dress on; except them."

"One could only imagine," DA said, shaking his head.

"Where was it located?" DA asked, in calmer tone.

"Beverly Hills, Bel Aire area," the coroner said, shrugging his shoulders in disappointment for not being able to furnish an address. "I never got an invite."

DA studied the coroner for a second before turning, grabbing the door knob and opening the door.

"Young man," the coroner called out. "Do you plan to kill me?"

DA never turned around to face the pleading men. He walked through the door and closed it behind himself. DA headed back to the others, it was time to conference and endure one more search.

Everyone that conspired to kill his parents would face the same inevitability; their own death. DA was certain the Fince brothers were guilty. There were only a few puzzling questions left; time would surely provide an answer.

Chapter 17

Can't Let 'Em Do It

DA glanced around the conference room noticing the partial emptiness. Crafty and Bearilla sat huddled up in the far corner while Ronald and Brazy tapped away on the laptop keyboards.

"Anybody know where Belinda and Dana at?" DA asked.

"They bounced with Sharon," Brazy exclaimed, spinning in his chair from the laptop screen. "I heard 'em say sumthin' about talking to somebody."

DA sat down at the conference table, pulled his cellphone, prepared to dial a number and an incoming call flashed on his screen. It was Dana.

"Y'all good?" DA questioned, answering his phone with concern.

"Yeah we good big bruh," Dana confided. "We on our way to talk to moms. I just wanna ask her a few more questions."

"Make sure you ask her about a sister that worked at the bank with a lot of power," DA demanded. "That's our scorned Casper the ghost."

"Gotchu' big bruh," Dana acknowledged. "Holla at you when we finish."

"Watch ya'self," DA spoke, disconnecting the call. "Hey Ronald. See what you can find out about a white women's high society club called the Eastern star. It useta' be in the Beverly Hills, Bel Aire area."

"I got you," Ronald replied.

DA rose from his chair and walked out of the conference room. He had known that most of the group were out on individual missions but Elliot and Mike were somewhere on the premises; he was in search of them. He wanted to run a few ideas by the pair.

DA strolled down the long dreary hallways full of remnants from the old business to find the second floor was empty. He headed down to the first floor and walked the long hallways never finding the pair.

DA was a little pissed at himself for not starting his search from the top floor and working his way down. The countless stairs were starting to take a toll on him. DA arrived on the third and final floor, and took a quick breather while he looked at the numerous paths.

COP KILLAS II, RENEWED JUSTICE

The word no was yelled out as the sound of scuffling ensued. DA could hear two voices scream and yell at one another while the shuffling of old office equipment directed his route. He peeked in room after room as he hurried through the corridor. An office chair came sliding through a door ten feet in front of him. That was one of rooms where they housed weapons.

DA rushed into the room to find Mike attempting to pin Elliot against a wall and Elliot slamming Mike across a table.

"What da' fuck goin' on in here?" DA yelled.

"DA help me restrain Elliot," Mike Bawled, tussling vigorously with the irate Elliot. "The bastards beat his woman and little boy!"

"WHAT!!!" DA shrieked, joining the attempt to restrain Elliot.

"Imma kill all those sons of bitches," Elliot sobbed. "I swear to God. They're beating up little children now!"

"Can't let him do it!" Mike yelled, struggling.

"It's a trap Elliot!" DA warned, joining in the restraint effort and tugging at Elliot's arms from behind him. "They already suspect you guys, and you've been off the clock for how long now?

Think Elliot! We got the upper hand. We'll make them pay for everything."

"They left 'em in the park DA," Elliot murmured, lessening his resistance. "Beaten and bruised like animals. They raped my woman! What upper hand we got for that DA? It's time to make 'em pay."

"We got element of surprise," DA answered, boldly stepping away from the men. "They only suspect your group. They know nothing of us."

Elliot let Mike go and stood up straight. Mike rose from off the table and sat on it. Both men were regaining their wind as they focused on the staring DA.

"This is why I came to find you two," DA advised. "I need y'all help. It's time to start putting together a plan for the Fince brothers. Their deaths have to be one for the record books."

"I'm personally with tearing the two fucks to pieces," Elliot conveyed. "Limb from fucking limb."

DA walked out the door with his arm around Elliot as Mike followed them.

"We just a phone call away from the perfect revenge," DA chatted. "And the limb from limb idea, might j–u–s–t– become reality."

COP KILLAS II, RENEWED JUSTICE

DA was awaiting the word from the Bag brothers before they entered the final stages of planning. Until then he would let Elliot and Mike relieve their stress killing the coroner and John Whitecloud.

Chapter 18

Piggy Bank

Belinda pulled the truck to a stop in front of First Republic Bank. Sharon began calling mom to see if she was in her office. The phone rang three times with no answer. Sharon understood even at near closing time banks could still be busy. She called back and let the phone ring again.

"I wonder if she in there," Belinda uttered, staring out her window at the bank's entrance.

"She's in there," Dana responded. "Post up right here and give it a few more minutes."

"Look!" Belinda yelled, pointing her finger at the banks entrance. "That's Adam Fince right there!"

"Son of a bitch," Sharon exclaimed, watching Adam Fince get in the backseat of a car. "Damn sure is."

"Looks like he has two goons with him too," Belinda reported, watching the car merge into traffic.

"Question is," Dana suggested. "Fuck is he doing here?"

"Stay here," Sharon demanded, opening the truck door. "I'm going to run in and see if she in the bank. Keep the truck running."

Sharon slammed the truck's passenger door and dodged her way through traffic running across the street. She entered the bank and disappeared from view. Belinda and Dana sat anxiously anticipating Sharon's return.

Only seconds after Sharon disappeared in the bank screeching tires alerted Belinda and Dana to a car racing in the opposite direction, already across the light the car was rapidly disappearing.

"Damn! I couldn't tell if that was her," Dana said, turning to see fading lights.

"I couldn't make out the make or model of the car either," Belinda shared, not being able to catch a good description of the car.

The two women were at a lost as to what to do. They both screamed questions at each other trying to figure their next move. Sharon emerged from the bank in a hurry crossing all lanes of oncoming traffic. She made it to the truck, snatched opened the door and slid back into the seat.

"The lady closing the bank say we just missed her," Sharon spoke, getting comfortable in her seat. "Adam Fince came in pissed off and walked into mom's office. He slammed the door and his goons made sure she stayed out of ear's distance. Moms flew out of the office right after Adam Fince walked out. She said Moms looked real bothered by something when she left."

"That was her flying down the street!" Dana expressed, giving her speculation.

"She gotta bout a minute and half head start on us," Belinda uttered, hard shifting the truck into drive and making a U-turn through traffic.

Dana frantically tried to call Moms as they raced through traffic trying to catch up to her. The group figured Moms was heading home based on the direction of the speeding car with the screeching tires.

"She still not answering," Dana complained, experiencing a sudden shock to her mind.

Dana dismissed the thought and attempted to call Mom's cellphone again. Still no answer.

Mom's bank was only fifteen minutes from her home location so Dana stop trying to call. They would be at her home shortly. Belinda maneuvered the truck through traffic bobbing and weaving in and out of it while they discussed the possibilities of Adam Fince's visit.

COP KILLAS II, RENEWED JUSTICE

Dana called DA's phone to tell him about Adam Fince's visit to the bank. DA was just as surprised as the three ladies were. He ordered that they call him as soon as they finish talking to Moms.

Belinda pulled the truck into the circular driveway and her and Dana rushed out of the vehicle. Sharon ushered the two women to go and promised that she would be right behind them. Sharon wanted to make one call to check something out.

Mom's front door was slightly opened as the two women approached the top of the stairs. They quickly made their way inside calling out Mom's name.

The two women stopped in their track as they entered the kitchen. They were both taking by surprise at what they stumbled upon. A single gunshot turned their surprise into instant fear.

Chapter 19

Snatch & Grab

The Bag brothers informed DA that the reporter Steven White had fled town. His mail had stacked up over the past three weeks and there was no sign of him anywhere.

"There was a couple of undercovers watching his crib when we got there," Nap Bags told, taking a seat next to DA.

"They spot y'all?" DA asked, eyeing the returning group as they also took a seat at the table.

"Two flashes. It was all over," Fingers responded, kicking his feet up on the conference table. "Quick, clean and not a witness."

DA called Elliot and Mike over to the conference table and proposed that they start working on a final plan to catch the Fince brothers. The crew began scheming details amongst each other. Thirty minutes later the group adapted a plan that everyone was on board with.

"Blood if that shit work I'm bowing to you brothers," Bloodstone voiced, acknowledging the

COP KILLAS II, RENEWED JUSTICE

Bag brother's input. "That's some way out shit. I ain't neva seen nobody pull that type of shit off."

"I like that shit cuzz," Mayhem joined in. "When we doing this?"

"Right now," DA replied, rising from the table. "Let's get everything we need. I wanna be rolling in the next hour."

The group rose from the table to grab their equipment and ready themselves for their impending mission.

~

"Y'all checking this out," DA asked, over the radio, as Mike pulled the truck over.

"Yeah," Pocket's voice, shot back across the radio. "We got eyes on 'em."

"According to tonight's agenda he should be here. He's a key speaker tonight," Elliot said, spying as Mike parked the truck on the corner. "I hope these dudes know what they're doing. There's a lot of cops in there. One fuck up and it'll be a war getting them out."

"They can handle this," DA expressed, with confidence watching the Bag brothers exit their van, pull a vending machine from the side door and strolling into the Police League Headquarters.

"I can't believe they're walking in that bitch," Bloodstone revealed, in amazement. "Now that's what I call gettin' gangsta' blood."

The Police League's Headquarter building was a three story edifice. Darryl Fince's office was located on the third floor, the biggest corner office in the building.

The Bag brothers entered the building and headed straight for the front desk. Nap Bags approached the counter and handed the police guard a set of papers while Kid Bags held the machine balance on a dolly.

"It's an order of exchange for vending machine number 01777365," Nap Bags articulated, leaning on the counter. "The paperwork says it's located on the third floor."

The guard looked up briefly from the paper to study both men before tapping the keys to a computer. The guard peered the screen for a few seconds and handed Nap Bags back his papers. The guard retrieved a plastic card from beneath the counter and handed it Nap bags while pointing out directions to the elevator.

"I think Ethel makes the best Sweet Potato pie we ever had," Kid Bags conveyed, pushing the vending machine across the lobby floor towards the elevators.

"The best chicken and rice?" Nap Bags quizzed, pushing the elevator button.

"Hands down Terry from Jordan Downs. That-girl-could-cook!" Kid Bags replied. "The best steak and gravy?"

"Shonda off uh Pico. Remember I fell asleep on her kitchen floor," Nap Bags confided, laughing and holding the open elevator door. "Best action packed movie?"

"Oooh! That's a hard one," Kid bags admitted, maneuvering the machine onto the elevator as the cops already aboard made room. "Lethal Weapon with Jet Li."

"Not even close," Nap bags shot back. "Arnold Schwarzenegger in Collateral Damage. He went to another country by himself and killed up the whole rebel posse. Plus he destroyed their entire drug operation. All that was for family revenge."

"Yeah I agree," Kid Bags conceded, sitting the machine down squarely. "Third floor. Thank you officer. Best Stallone movie and/or series?"

"Rambo," Nap Bags stated.

"Cobra!" A cop interrupted, hearing the competitive quiz being shared between the brothers. The cop couldn't restrain himself; he was enjoying the challenge.

Both bag brothers turned to face the cop whose remark caught their attention. The brothers look between themselves and the cop two quick times before holding their stare at one another for a brief second.

"Yeahhh," the brothers agreed.

"The fight scene with the blade wielding maniac," Nap Bags said, exaggerating his excitement.

"That's the famous shivering lip scene," Kid Bags demonstrated, allowing his bottom lip to drop in the corner while he acted out the stress filled scene.

The cops began laughing at the comedic brother's gestures. The elevator door opened exposing the second floor and two officer stepped off laughing. The doors closed and the brothers picked up right where they left off at as the elevator headed upwards to the third and final floor.

"Best horror flick?" Nap Bags asked.

"Poltergeist!" The officer announced, trying to beat Kid Bags' answer.

Both brothers stared at one another again momentarily before giving a simultaneous glance to the officer and back to one another.

"Yeahhh," the brother sang, in unison smiling at the cop and giving slaps to his shoulder.

The elevator doors opened and the cop stepped out first wishing the brothers a good night as he turned the corner and disappeared. The brothers stared at one another with sly smirks.

Nap Bags held the door while his brother Kid dragged the machine off the elevator and followed his brother down the hallway.

"Best comedy and/or series?" Kid Bags asked, dropping the machine next to the other vending machine and unlocking it.

Kid Bags moved to the other machine, unlocked it and starting removing its contents, placing them on the floor while Nap bags pulled a bag from the inside of the machine they brought in.

"You already know I'm going with Friday," Nap Bags responded, checking the handle of the office door to see if it was locked. "Ice Cube made a classic with that one. It's open," he whispered.

"Here," Kid Bags exclaimed, handing Nap Bags a rag as he stepped in the office.

"I'll be back in two snaps," Nap Bag disclosed, letting the door close slowly and quietly on its own. "Janitorial."

Kid Bags closed the door of the vending machine and tilted it on a dolly. With a quick spin maneuver he placed the machine perfectly aligned with Darryl Fince's office. Kid bags opened the door to the machine again, stepped away and loaded the first machine back to its capacity with the exception of one chocolate candy bar, placed neatly on the floor, squared in the middle of the machine.

It was just mere seconds before the light sounds of a rumble could be heard by Kid Bags. Kid Bags moved back to the machine with its door open and held it steady while observing the hallway.

The office door clicked opened and Nap Bags emerged with an unconscious Fince inside of a laundry bag being dragged directly from the floor to the inside of the machine. Only Fince's head was visible. Darryl Fince's eye was swollen and he bled from his mouth as his body slumped in confinement within the machine. Nap Bags closed the office door, then the machine's door. Kid Bags tilted the machine back onto the dolly and the brothers headed back to the elevator.

The ex-chief was being paged via intercom as the brothers entered the elevator and pushed the button for the first floor. The door closed.

~

"They've been in there for a while now," Bloodstone told, sounding slightly concerned watching the constant flow of officers entering the garage level and street level of the edifice.

"It hasn't been ten minutes yet," DA spoke, checking the time on his watch. "They'll be out. Give 'em a few minutes."

According to DA's synchronized watch a little more than six minutes had passed.

The crew sat in the truck quietly for the next few minutes watching more officers pour into the building.

"It's pass ten minutes," Elliot said, opening back up the discussion. "And we closing in on the twelve minute mark real fast."

DA turned in his seat about to speak when Bloodstones' excitement broke his thought.

"There they go blood!" Bloodstone yelled. "There they go! They pulled that shit off!"

The crew watched as the two brothers emerged from the building, strolling through the crowd of entering cops; seemingly invisible. The brothers could be seen chatting as they made their way back to the van.

The brothers loaded the vending machine into the van, closed the door and slid in the front seats. With a flash of the van's rear lights Mike pulled away from the curb and pulled closely behind the van. Crafty pulled his truck out front of the van and the group carefully caravanned away.

COP KILLAS II, RENEWED JUSTICE

Chapter 20

Snakes In The Grass

Dana sat befuddled as to what was going on. She and Belinda walked in to find Adam Fince and Ms. Williams engaged in a loving embrace.

Dana was shocked watching Ms. Williams pull a small caliber pistol and firing one shot into Belinda's chest and even more shocked when Ms. Williams pointed her weapon in Dana's direction.

"What the fuck you doing?" Dana questioned, looking completely stunned as two men appeared directly behind her.

The two men restrained Dana grabbing her by both arms. With a shove in the back Dana was pushed further in the kitchen as Adam Fince slid a chair in her direction.

"Strap her down," Adam Fince ordered.

The two men tied Dana to a chair with rope provided by Ms. Williams as Belinda's body laid in the kitchen doorway.

"Get her out of here," Adam Fince ordered, his two goons who had finished confining Dana to the chair. "The visual image of someone dying is such an unpleasant sight."

The two goons dragged Belinda's body into another room while Adam took his stance next to Ms. Williams.

"What da' fuck?" Dana uttered, struggling to break free. "You working for this muthafuckin' devil?"

"Working with is more like it," Sharon replied, entering the kitchen and grabbing a bottled water from the refrigerator. "But don't worry, you'll find out everything soon enough."

"Oh you working with these muthafuckas too?" Dana turned, staring at Sharon slamming the refrigerator door.

"Y'all two dead bitches!" Dana yelled, trying to figure this connection.

"You know you sound exactly like your mother," Ms. Williams confided, rubbing Dana's cheek and then slapping her face so hard that spit flew from her mouth. "And I couldn't stand that bitch either."

"I got some news for you though," Sharon interrupted, giving Ms. Williams a kiss on the cheek. "Moms is my biological mother. I couldn't believe you and DA couldn't see the resemblance."

COP KILLAS II, RENEWED JUSTICE

Dana sat spellbound for a moment looking back and forth between the two women.

"Oh I see it now," Dana expressed, with a chuckle. "Both you bitches look like snakes!"

"Well she definitely is her mother's child?" Adam Fince teased, moving in for a closer inspection of Dana. "And where's this brother of hers? I'm going to assume he's like his father."

"Yeah he is," Dana retorted, spitting in Adam Fince's direction. "There's just one tiny difference."

"What's that young lady?" Adam Fince asked.

"My brother's going to kill you," Dana shot back, with a smile of her own.

Adam Fince laughed off the threat and turned back towards Ms. Williams.

"Linda I must say this was truly a great plan," Adam Fince spoke, kissing Ms. Williams' cheek. "You know I have always had faith in you."

"I only wish that your brother shared in your faith," Ms. Williams spoke, taking a seat at the table.

"Don't worry about him. He's under control," Adam Fince notified.

"Ok. Then it's time to bring this tale to a final conclusion," Ms. Williams said. "Sharon make the call."

"Yes mama," Sharon answered, pulling her cellphone and starting her walk out of the room. "Hey where's Belinda?"

"We dragged her into the garage after Ms. Williams shot her," One goon replied.

"Shot her where?" Sharon asked, suspiciously.

"Right where you're standing," the other goon informed.

"No idiot. Where did my mama shoot her?" Sharon requested, tapping several spots across her chest.

"I shot her in the chest," Ms. Williams told, with emphasis.

"The bitch wearing a bullet proof vest," Sharon communicated, shaking her head while exposing her own vest and storming out of the kitchen.

Adam Fince ordered his goons to follow and help Sharon properly dispose of Belinda.

Ms. Williams went into a blank stare flabbergasted by the new tale of events. She soon turned her glare to Dana.

COP KILLAS II, RENEWED JUSTICE

"Did y'all find out yet?" Ms. Williams inquired, staring at Dana.

"Find out what bitch?" Dana snapped.

"That I'm the one who had your parents killed," Ms. Williams conveyed.

Dana sat with the look of murder written across her face while Ms. Williams taunted her with words meant to destroy. The news blew Dana away.

"Me and your mother were never friends," Ms. Williams began. "That bitch stole my man…and that weak ass daddy of yours, ohh I wish I could have killed him personally. He was so fucking weak; he disgusted me."

"I'm pretty sure you disgusted him more," Dana shot back. "You disgust the shit outta me. I can't stand the sight of you bitch. But I assure you, you getting *Fucked Up!*"

Ms. Williams smirked and picked up where she left off.

"He was sleeping with me and Diane at the same time but Diane fortunately got pregnant with Darryl Junior," Ms. Williams told. "Once that nosey bitch you call Aunt Betty snitched about me and Darryl's relationship, yo' sad ass mama used her pregnancy as a control mechanism; but I had a plan for that and simple ass bitch. I fed a few people some insight; your parents for example, and that started the ball rolling. All I had to do then was sit back and let nature take its course."

"Rotten ass bitch," Dana uttered.

"I agree. Your mama was a rotten ass bitch," Ms. Williams apprised, with a growing smile on her face. "Nothing ass bitch! Thought she really was somebody, once Darryl got her a job in his office. All of a sudden she developed this high and mighty attitude like she was better than everybody else; like she was better than me! I showed her ass though."

"We got a problem," Sharon cried, rushing back into the kitchen. "Belinda gone!"

"Dammit!" Adam Fince screamed, rising from his seat. "Where are my men at?"

"They're out trying to find her," Sharon responded. "She couldn't have gone too far."

The two henchmen entered the kitchen just a minute later in haste, out of breath, and embarrassed. One of them stepped forward.

"She got away in a truck that was parked out in the driveway," The goon spoke.

COP KILLAS II, RENEWED JUSTICE

Adam Fince snapped his fingers pointing to the door and moved towards the kitchen's exit.

"I'd advise you to clean this mess up expeditiously," Adam Fince warned, Ms. Williams. "I'll call you with the contact location as soon as possible."

Adam Fince and his men vanished quickly, disappearing from the home.

Chapter 21

Change of Plans

DA attempted again and again to contact all three women; neither woman answered the call.

"Nobody answering?" Pockets asked, starting to worry. "My baby don't ignore my calls and I called her three times; three times DA! Something's wrong."

Let's not start jumping to conclusions," DA advised, worrying himself. "They'll be calling soon."

It had been over an hour since they had heard from Belinda, Dana or Sharon. Pockets continued to pace the floor back and forth while the looked on with discernment.

"DA, try Moms again," Pockets counselled. "See if she heard from them."

DA figured it to be a waste of time. He had called Ms. Williams at the bank and at home with no response.

DA looked down at his phone as it began to ring and vibrate on the table. He glanced at the caller ID and pushed the talk button.

COP KILLAS II, RENEWED JUSTICE

"Where y'all at?" DA inquired, listening intently.

The voice on the phone began talking with sounds of desperation while DA's face showed the signs of confusion.

"What? You ok? Moms! Where you at?" DA questioned.

The voice continued to speak at a fast pace. DA continued to listen intently while the voice continued to inform.

"You sure?" DA demanded, listening a few more seconds before interrupting. "We'll meet you there as soon as possible."

DA disconnected the call and informed the group of the latest development. The entire group was stunned and dumbfounded.

They were checking their weapons when his phone rang again. DA looked at his caller ID again and pushed the talk button.

The voice came through the line and immediately initiated a high speed talk.

"Fince!" DA screamed into the phone. "Where's Dana?"

The voice continued to share their story.

"Where you at now?" DA asked.

"Meet up with Mike and them. We on the way," DA yelled, into the phone before disconnecting the call in a hurry.

"We got problems," DA notified, the group. "Grab that muthafucka Fince, load up and let's roll! We'll discuss the new plan while we rolling."

COP KILLAS II, Renewed Justice

Chapter 22

It's on & Poppin'

DA sat in the passenger seat of the truck thinking to himself about what he had just learned via the two phone calls he received. DA sent a crew to retrieve Belinda and rendezvous with them at the designated location.

Pockets sat in the second rows of seats next to Darryl Fince severely agitated.

"Anything happens to my girl and I swear to you I'm cutting your nuts off and feeding you both of 'em," Pockets promised, poking his sharp blade into the side of Darryl Fince. "You understand me pig?"

Darryl Fince grunted a little but refused to acknowledge Pockets' threat and promise. Fince simply stared in the face of his captor.

"All of you niggers are going to die tonight," Darryl Fince uttered, fearlessly with a slight smile. "You won't be getting away with this one."

"My bad. I forgot to tell you. I'm the official round here. Pockets please instruct the prisoner to shut da' fuck up?" DA asked, looking over his shoulder at Darryl Fince.

Pockets quickly turned facing Darryl Fince and punched him squarely in the eye causing it to swell and blacken almost immediately. Pockets threw a couple more punches to face and head of Darryl Fince as he groaned loudly. Darryl Fince was left gasping for breath.

"We already have our hands on you. Now shut yo' muthafuckin' ass up klan; fo' I kill you," Pockets warned. "Ain't nobody playing witcho' punk ass. Ain't nobody playing witcho' punk ass!"

Crafty and the Bag brothers rode in silence while Pockets continued to make Darryl Fince feel the reality of his current predicament.

They were nearing fifteen minutes away when DA's phone buzzed through a text message. DA read and responded to the message with a smile and gave a nod of his head.

Crafty pulled the Suburban into the parking lot of the National Guard's Armory facility sixteen minutes later. The crew spied the surrounding entrance as they passed through it.

"Hold up here Crafty," DA cautioned, checking his buzzing phone's text message while keeping a steady eye on the environment. "Take off Crafty but keep an eye out for anything funny. Pockets come with me. If you don't hear from either of us in five minutes Nat, put a bullet in Mr. Fince's head. We'll hook up at your location."

"Be careful bruh," Crafty warned, pulling the Suburban truck out of the parking lot.

DA and Pockets stepped out of the vehicle and began their stroll through the corridor of buildings searching the roofs and corners of the buildings as they passed.

The corridor was a long strip of gigantic seven foot tall cement square flower pots that housed beautiful ten foot tall palm trees in two rows. DA and Pockets walked between the two rows until they neared the huge steps that led to a wide platform that served as an entrance to an unlit building.

DA began calling out loud.

A voice with a loud echo coming from the dark answered back instructing the two to stop where they stood. The voice sounded feminine.

"Where's my sister Sharon?" DA asked, unsurprised by the betrayal.

"Where's my woman bitch?" Pockets screamed, in succession.

"She's present!" Sharon barked, emerging from the darkness of the building to the partially lit platform dragging a cuffed Dana along.

"Right here Big Bruh! I'm right here boo!" Dana announced, struggling like a bonafide soldier with her plastic tie cuffs.

Dana's eyes told of the trust, solidarity, devotion and love she shared with Pockets. Their love was a celestial one.

"In public baby?" Pockets pleaded. 'C'mon baby not in public. You promised you wouldn't call me boo in public."

"I'm sorry boo," Dana said. "But dis' bitch got a gun at the side of my head. You know how I get when I get emotional."

"You know I'm gon' kill that bitch? Right baby," Pocket asked, rhetorically.

"I know my little psycho," Dana teased, in the mist of force from Sharon's pistol pushing head trauma.

"It would only be befitting that you two die together. I been tired of the Bonni & Clyde love story bullshit for quite some time." Sharon spoke, stepping into the light and shoving Dana in a directed path with her pistol shoved against Dana's head. "Killing this sad romance bullshit is a thankful extra. Sorry Pockets! Besides the love shit all of y'all are actually cool. Sorry to you too DA, you were a bomb ass lover."

"So it's true," DA announced, glancing over at Pockets unsurprised. "But why though?"

Mrs. Williams strutted up the corridor just in time to hear DA's question.

"Cause Mama's always right," Ms. Williams interjected, stepping into sight brandishing her own pistol as Sharon's smile brightened.

"Mama has always known that her past would come back to haunt her at some time," Sharon conveyed. "So like any true thinker she devised a plan that worked like a c-h-a-r-m.

"Mama!" Pockets shouted, in disbelief. "That bitch yo' mama too."

"I got another 'A-r-m' word for you," DA interrupted. "Karma! And yo' ass getting a strong dose of her tonight. A strong dose bitch."

"Did you ever find the responsible party who guided your thirst for revenge?" Sharon questioned, with the air of superiority. "The one who caused you to revisit the horrid nightmares of watching your uncle die. The same one who guided you to the truth about the death of your parents. You probably guessed it by now. Yeah, it was mama."

"And thanks to you DA," Ms. Williams stated. "You have successfully killed 99 percent of my enemies in your skillful and magnificent quest to avenge the loss of your family. Unfortunate for you though, you're either going to jail tonight hunny or you're going to be killed standing right there."

Adam Fince walked into the picture assuring DA, Dana and Pockets that they would be experiencing significant pain either way.

Adam seemed to carry a look of worry across his face as he pushed a button on his phone and waited for a response. He dropped his phone to his side and continued to give his threats as he patted Sharon on the shoulder.

"Thanks to some great police work by Officer Brown here, whom I'm sure will someday be the first black female chief of LAPD, we have you for the numerous murders of police officials," Adam Fince told, with a slight laughter under his tone. "It'll be wonderful watching cop killers like you get the needle. I'll be informing my brother of your identity and guilt soon enough."

"I can promise you that bitch ass brother of yours won't be getting that message," DA spoke, with his own laughter growing with Pockets. "I hope that wasn't who you were trying to reach just now."

"Believe me," Pockets joined in, still laughing. "He's currently in a meeting and won't be able to available to attend tonight's festivities."

DA looked over at Pockets incredulously. Both men shared a hefty laugh.

"What DA?" Pockets Questioned, quickly. "Stop acting like I ain't got no vocabulary. Stop acting like it."

DA didn't say a word. He refocused his attention to Adam Fince.

Adam Fince pushed a button on his phone frantically and awaited an answer; none came. He pushed another button and waited again.

"Hello!" Adam responded, to the voice answering the call. "This is Adam Fince. Is my brother in attendance tonight?"

The voice had confirmed Darryl Fince's disappearance saying that he was certain of his arrival here earlier but suddenly vanished right before it was time for him to address the attendees. Adam disconnected the call.

"Stalemate dumbass," Pockets stated. "Stalemate!"

"Not quite yet," Adam Fince combatted, giving a whistle and watching shadowy figures emerge from the roofs of two buildings. His laugh was loud and continuous now.

DA and Pockets scanned the roof tops. There were twelve unidentifiable figures who had taken position on the two roofs. DA glanced over at Pockets winking his right eye at him.

"This seems more like a check mate to me son," Adam Fince bragged. "Now where's my brother?"

"He's close by," DA announced. "But his well-being depends on you."

"He's bluffing Adam!" Ms. Williams urged. "Don't buy his bullshit! Your brother is probably dead already!"

"Yeah!" Sharon added. "Don't trust 'em!"

DA drew his phone, made a call and placed the speaker on loud. Nap Bags answered.

"They wanna hear the bitch," DA told.

COP KILLAS II, Renewed Justice

"Kill 'em all!" Darryl Fince screamed, quickly through the line before the phone was snatched away and his voice muffled.

DA place his phone in his pocket and stared Adam Fince in his eyes with death.

"I promise to fulfill your wish brother!" Adam Fince yelled out in reply. "I want my brother standing here besides me in the next 88 seconds or every one and of you, and-I-mean-every-one-of-you-niggers will be executed on goddamn spot! Do-you-understand-me-boy? Am I being fucking understood?"

"Yeah we clear," DA submitted, turning his face to the right to look Pockets in the eye. "Pockets, go get dat cracka. You'll have to excuse him while he gets that bitch of a brother of yours."

DA returned his face to the sight of Adam Fince while Pockets acknowledged the demand.

"Fa sho! Fa sho!" Pockets obeyed, turning and strolling back towards the entrance. His exit was made hearing the last words of Dana.

DA! This bitch ain't our mother," Dana blurted out. "She's the one that orchestrated the death of our mama! And daddy!"

"Subject is moving," One hooded figure announced, via silent ear radio.

"Unit one covering. Copy?" Another figure replied, touching his ear as he and one more began to move following the subject.

"Maintain radio contact," The commander ordered. "Cover subject."

"Copy," The hooded figure acknowledged, staying in tow.

The men followed Pockets to a neighboring five story parking garage where they lost sight of their target as he entered the structure.

"Hustle," One figure said, to another jumping from top of the building to the roof of an army truck.

One man ran across the street while the other monitored his partner's movement through the scope of his rifle from the end of the roof he was already on.

"Subject entering elevator," The following figure informed.

"We won't have sight depending on what level subject gets off on," The stationary figure warned.

"Advise," The following figure asked, huddling in the bushes spying the first floor.

"Follow with caution. Report your 20," the stationary figure replied, searching the area with a quick eye inspection. "I'm searching for higher ground."

"Copy," The following figure acknowledged, before scaling the mid-level wall and disappearing into the structure.

~

Kid Bags received the radio transmission from Pockets as Pockets entered the Armory's parking lot.

Kid nodded at Nap, opened the back door, touch Crafty's shoulder over the seat, grabbed his bag and stepped out of the vehicle.

"They come out that door or up that ramp, you run a muthafucka over to get to that bottom. I'll meet you there," Kid Bags instructed.

Kid Bags slammed the door and ran over to the dark far near corner of the north side of the structure. He quickly connected the Wilson suppressor to his automatic weapon and studied the Armory's parking lot. He spotted Pockets walking through the parking lot and nearing its exit. Soon after, he sighted both of Pockets' followers and conveyed his findings to Pockets.

"Your right," Kid Bags conveyed, looking through his scope. "There's exactly two of them following along the roof top. I got 'em. One of 'em just jump down to a truck and is currently creeping behind you, on foot."

"I'll take him at the top," Pockets radioed back, now crossing the street "You take the other one. Mr. Nap get Darryl Fince ready."

"He's in place," Nap Bags radioed in. "Waiting on you."

Kid studied the movements of both men. He watched the first man huddling against the wall while the other seemed to be searching for a better and higher view without blowing his cover. The man settled for the fire escape laddering on the adjoining building. The building had enough height to give him the vision he needed to observe the parking garage roof. The figure began climbing. Kid Bag took careful aim and waited for the figure to finish his climb. The figure settle on top and touched his ear with his hand.

~

"I got your cover," the figure warned, studying the roof's entrance.

"Following subject up stairwell," The following figure told. "Will advise. Copy."

"Copy that," The stationary figure acknowledged, spying through the lens of his scope at the parked black SUV.

The spying sniper adjusted his scope to better his view of what looked like two men; one shielded by the truck's door.

"We have a positive ID of Darryl Fince commander. Copy?" The spying sniper indicated, maneuvering his rifle from Darryl Fince back across the rooftop. "Oh fuck!"

"Unit two enroute to you," The commander's voice replied. "What's your position?"

~

Kid Bags watched the sniper catch a glimpse of Darryl Fince, touch his ear, talk and begin his search of the rest of the roof.

"Good night," Kid Bags whispered, watching the sniper's head jerk back from shock of being spotted first.

Kid Bags' one shot tore through the forehead of the spying sniper killing him instantly.

"Man down," Kid bags uttered, into his radio.

~

Pockets reached the top floor of the garage and pushed the heavy metal door open letting it slam close on its own; he took his position in the far corner and cocked his pistol's hammer back.

The following figure rushed to the door and halted communicating through his ear piece. His partner hadn't returned the commander's request and he was trying to ascertain his next order when he felt a sudden calmness overcome him.

The figure slowly turned his head to witness the pistol flash that ended his life. Pockets had stepped behind the figure aiming his gun at the back of the man's head. The figure slowly turned his head to a perfect side shot, his body now stretched across the threshold of the door.

Pockets stepped over the figure's body pushing the door open and adjusted his sight directly in front of himself. Nap Bags stood with a pistol to Darryl Fince's head.

"Let's go," Pockets called out, holding the door open while Nap Bags pushed Darryl Fince in his direction.

Nap Bags grabbed his rifle and headed to the opposite corner of the roof from his brother. Both Bag brothers took aim across the street as Pockets escorted Darryl Fince back across the Armory's parking lot.

The Bag brothers took swift and deadly action at the sight of Unit Two moving along the roof in search of Unit One. Two muffled sounds fired off at nearly the same time stopping the two men of Unit Two. Unit Two's bodies were sprawled out along the rooftop.

~

Pockets walked back across the parking lot with Darryl Fince slow dragging in front.

"Keep it moving!" Pockets ordered. "I should pop yo' ass right now. I heard about you, Simon and them little boys; nasty muthafuckas."

"We woulda' had a ball with your little black ass," Darryl shot back, trying to quickly tuck his head like a turtle in a failing attempt to miss Pockets' oncoming pistol strike to his head.

"Say some more gay shit like dat and see if I don't lay yo' ass out where you stand," Pockets warned, kicking the crouching Darryl Fince in the ass. "Walk muthafucka!"

Darryl Fince stumbled scurrying along as Pockets took notice that no one was following him this time. He peered at the roof top time and time again as he and his captive neared the entrance to the corridors. The light sounds of talk grew louder as Pockets pushed Darryl Fince in the direction of DA and his brother Adam's conversation.

"One thing I can assure you Mr. Fince," DA started. "Regardless of what happens here tonight, I promise you, you're leaving here in a body bag. Now that's something you can take to the bank."

DA studied the roof top detecting the assassin's apparent confusion.

"We'll, it seems we finally have our awaited company," Adam Fince roared, gleefully at the sight of his brother and captor nearing. "I guess we can get this show on the road now."

"Brother for sister," DA demanded. "Let her walk and we let him do the same."

"I'm sorry to spoil your plans of controlling this situation young man," Adam Fince stated, with an evil smirk turning to look at Sharon. "But you're either going to let my brother go or I'm going to order Officer Sharon Brown here to put a bullet in that bitch's head. Your call; and you don't have all day."

Sharon cocked back on the pistol's hammer forcing Dana's head to tilt sideways as she grunted.

"Just shoot the bitch!" Ms. Williams yelled, with a growing rage. "I'm tired of all this talk!"

DA gave a head nod and Pockets gave Darryl Fince a push in the back.

Darryl Fince commenced walking towards his brother with slow steps as he looked backwards over his shoulder at the untrusted Pockets mean mugging him.

A single shot broke the temporary silence and caused Darryl Fince to crouch and most to jump.

Everyone began looking around for the culprit and victim. No one seemed to have gotten hit until Darryl Fince's crouch position became a sprawled out display. The back corner of his head was gushing out blood like a fountain. Nap Bags was spotted on an adjoining roof giving his one finger salute before him and Kid Bags turned their guns on the assassins.

Pockets without further hesitation drew his weapon and fired one shot directly into the mouth of Sharon, killing her instantly and knocking her backwards away from Dana. Sharon's body smashed against the cement floor releasing her grip of the pistol she held.

The pistol slid in the direction of Adam Fince who rushed to retrieve it. Dana ducked her head low and took off running zig zag down the stairs in the direction of Pockets.

Ms. Williams started squeezing off shots of her own in the direction of the fleeing Dana, DA and Pockets as she covered Adam Fince's maneuver to grab Sharon's gun.

"You killed my daughter you son of a bitch!" Ms. Williams screamed, continuing to fire off shots.

Pockets returned fire covering Dana's escape.

DA leaned behind the flower pot grabbing his shoulder. A bullet from Ms. Williams' gun found its mark there.

Dana made it into the arms of Pockets who in one fluid motion spent her behind the cement flower pot next to DA, leaned in kissing her deep and passionately. Pockets pulled his knife from his pocket, cut Dana's hands free and pulled his lips from hers beginning to recite his love for her.

"Will you two knock it off? This ain't the time or place for dat' shit," DA yelled, observing the assassins on the roof engaging in their own fire fight against the Bag brothers and the others.

Dana took a moment to glance at DA and give him a hug.

"DA you bleeding!" Dana yelled, checking her brother's arm.

"It's okay baby girl," DA returned, quickly hugging his baby sister and peeking out to see Ms. Williams and Adam Fince escaping through the building. "It just ripped the flesh a little. C'mon we have to catch those two!"

DA face showed the expression of death's executioner as he took off after the fleeing duo. Pockets handed Dana a gun as the two caught up to DA entering the building in pursuit.

"Oooooh," Dana growled, in stride. "I hope I get dis' bitch."

~

"You witnessing this shit?" Mike asked, peering through the binoculars.

The Bag brothers, Crafty, Bearilla, Ronald, Brazy, Mayhem, Fingers and Bloodstone had taken the fight to the roof mounted assassins.

"Yeah," Elliot answered, tugging Belinda's shoulder. "And I'll be damn if Fince is getting away."

DA's group approached from two directions forcing some of the assassins to jump from the roof to ground level.

"Y'all go help DA and them," Mike ordered. "I'm going to join in the gun battle."

The gun battle was a fierce one that lasted several minutes. Mike's ground level entrance attack from behind allowed the group an opportunity to dismount the roof and crush the assassins' stance.

~

COP KILLAS II, RENEWED JUSTICE

DA, Dana and Pockets stayed close to the hallways walls as they peeked in every room they passed with guns ready. Ms. Williams and Adam Fince seemingly vanished from sight upon entering the building. The trio knew they were lurking someone near. Their jog became a slow walk as they visually inspected everything in their path. They made it to the end of the hallway with no sighting of the fleeing pair.

Pockets quick peek around the corner of the hallway was greeted with three quick shots in sequence. The first shot nearly ripping through his face.

"Dat bitch! Dat bitch!" Pockets screamed, tucking his head firmly against the wall. "We gotta whoop her ass first."

~

"They're closing in fast," Adam Fince spoke, nearly out of breath and bent over with his palms resting his arms on his knees. "We won't make it without stalling them."

Ms. Williams fired a few more shots off. Her gun began clicking; it was empty. Adam Fince realized her gun had no more bullets and stuck his own pistol out the door way squeezing off shots.

"I have a fresh clip," Adam Fince conveyed. "I'll hold them off while you get to the car. Blow the horn once you make it. I'll be there momentarily."

Ms. Williams kissed Adam Fince's lips and headed for the exit that was located twenty feet away. She disappeared through the door and Adam Fince fired more shots down the hallway.

"Your identity is known son," Adam Fince yelled out. "You're getting the death penalty for this."

"How?" DA blurted. "Neither one of y'all making it out of here alive. Whose gon' know?"

Adam Fince made a soft backwards peddle towards the exit while he and DA communicated. The horn sounded off and Adam Fince's gun blazed again as he ran for the exit.

The crew noticed the sudden quietness from Adam Fince after the horn blowing. Pockets peeked around the corner again.

"Aghh! These muthafuckas getting away," Pockets screamed, heading around the corner and down the hall. "C'mon!"

COP KILLAS II, RENEWED JUSTICE

DA, Dana and Pockets made it outside just in time to see Ms. Williams screeching the tires of the Mercedes Benz away and towards the exit.

"Fuck!" DA yelled, pulling his cell phone from his pocket as he watched the Benz speeding through the exit.

Dana and Pockets fired shot after shot at speeding vehicle unable to halt its getaway. The Benz was making a left turn out of the exit when its rear panel was smacked hard, nearly head on by a black Suburban truck.

"Ooooh Shit!" the crew murmured, in unison as they began running towards the accident.

The Suburban slammed on its brakes screeching to a stop while the Benz went spinning towards the sidewalk. Ms. Williams and Adam Fince were incoherent as they both bobbed around in their seat. The Benz ended up crashing its opposite rear side panel into the corner of an old brick building; the Benz was disabled.

Elliot and Belinda emerged from the undamaged black Suburban making a bee line for the Benz.

Before DA, Dana and Pockets could get there Elliot and Belinda had shattered both driver and passenger windows, forcibly removing both occupants with choke holds.

The beat down that Adam Fince and Ms. Williams were receiving was visually stimulating to the oncoming trio. They could hear the repetition of lines being spoken by both Belinda and Elliot as they pounded away bare fisted on the faces of Adam Fince and Ms. Williams.

"This is for trying to kill me bitch!" Belinda yelled, continuously as she continued to punch Ms. Williams in the face. "This is for trying to kill me bitch!"

"This is for my woman!" Elliot screamed, punching Adam Fince as hard as he could, repeatedly in the ribs and face. "This is for my boy!"

DA, Dana and Pockets rested at the crash site. Neither one uttered a word of interruption. It was like it was telepathically agreed upon; 'let 'em put some work in.'

The rest of DA's team showed up at the beat down sight and gathered around the scene. DA gave Crafty and Bearilla a head nod, and the two began to pull Elliot and Belinda off their victims.

"Baby Girl you wanna finish this bitch off," DA asked, cocking his pistol and glancing over at Adam Fince.

Dana walked over to the barely recognizable Ms. Williams who had started her whining pleas. Dana was deaf to every word she spoke as she ejected her clip to check it before slapping it back in. She had almost a full clip.

"To hell with the record books," Elliot murmured, pulling his pistol and firing off shots as he walked to a standing position over Adam Fince's body.

The crew looked on as Elliot emptied his gun into the body of Adam Fince who was now dead for sure.

"That's for my little man who you had beaten and left in the park with his raped mother," Elliot spoke, calmly eyeing the lifeless body of Adam Fince. "You dead son of a bitch."

DA and the crew turned their attention back to Dana who again was focusing on Ms. Williams. Ms. Williams began her begging immediately.

"Please don't kill me!" Ms. Williams mumbled, nearly out of breath. "I can help you run this city. You can do whatever you want. Just let me help you DA. You can be the man just like your father wanted for you. I can guide you there DA."

"Bitch!" Dana yelled, snatching the rifle from Mike's hands, pulling the clip out and ejecting the chambered round. "The only one being guided around here is you. I'm finna' guide yo' ass to the other side; slow and painfully."

A final plea of 'Nooo!' was heard from Ms. Williams. Dana's barrage of rifle butt blows to Ms. Williams' head and body muffled her screams.

Belinda rejoined the attack with her own rifle butt pounding away on Ms. Williams' disfigured face and body. The two women beat Ms. Williams for several minutes until she had visibly stopped breathing as they crew watched on.

Belinda squatted checking with two fingers to the bloody neck of Ms. Williams and returned her gaze with a look of certainty as she stood, nodding her head in confirmation of death. Ms. Williams was gone. Dana finalized the motion sending two shells from a pistol into the skull of Ms. Williams.

"Now she's confirmed dead!" Dana declared.

The crew looked in one another eyes momentarily and began loading up into their trucks. They drove away with a sense of accomplishment. They had truly renewed justice.

COP KILLAS II, Renewed Justice

www.ingramcontent.com/pod-product-compliance
Lightning Source LLC
Chambersburg PA
CBHW071313250626
47159CB00004B/1410